THREE PROMISES

Also by Bishop O'Connell

The Stolen
The Forgotten

THREE PROMISES

An American Faerie Tale Collection

BISHOP O'CONNELL

HARPER
VOYAGER
IMPULSE

An Imprint of HarperCollinsPublishers

This is a work of fiction. Names, characters, places, and incidents are products of the author's imagination or are used fictitiously and are not to be construed as real. Any resemblance to actual events, locales, organizations, or persons, living or dead, is entirely coincidental.

Lyrics to "Wonder (Wonder Woman Song)" used by permission of The Doubleclicks.

EPub Edition DECEMBER 2015 ISBN: 9780062449849

Print Edition ISBN: 9780062449856

10 9 8 7 6 5 4 3 2 1

CONTENTS

CONTENTS

For "The Boot" and Dennis Morgan.

For the fans who waited so patiently (you did wait patiently, right?) to learn what happened to Brendan.

To Ed and Lee Ann, I wish you both the greatest happiness in your new life together.

And for Geofferson Ray Loughery, my newest fan. Though your parents should wait until you're a little older before reading this book to you . . . like two.

AUTHOR'S NOTE

There's a saying in the military that no battle plan survives first contact with the enemy. For me, the same is true with my writing. No outline survives the first few chapters; new characters are created and take on a life of their own, side plots and stories emerge that beg to be told. Sometimes they're just flourishes that can be stored away, or ignored as unimportant. But others are more insistent and just won't be silent. These are those stories. They needed to be told. They give you a deeper insight into the American Faerie Tale universe and let you see beyond the confines of the story line that birthed them. You won't need to have read *The Stolen* and/or *The Forgotten* to enjoy these pieces. If this is your first book in the American Faerie Tale world, I hope you enjoy these glimpses into the lives of characters that I love writing about so much. Fair warning, there are spoilers in these stories if you haven't read the first two books. And if you have read the other books, I hope you enjoy this deeper look at the characters that make up that magical world.

The first promise, "The Legacy of Past Promises," is a sort of origin story for Elaine (introduced in *The Forgotten*). It explains why she's no longer a noble amongst the fae, and where her distrust of the fae courts comes from. I was delighted to really explore her story and let it, and her, be everything they could be. Timeline wise, it's set about six months before the beginning of *The Forgotten*.

The second promise is "The Promise of New Beginnings." I admit my stories tend to have a touch of the bittersweet to them, but if any story deserves an unapologetic happy ending, it's a wedding story. I love Edward and Caitlin; and their wedding, though far from perfect, was something I really wanted to share with my readers. In this story you'll get some deeper insights into the two unlikely loves, and perhaps will even see them in a new light. This story takes places a few months after the end of *The Forgotten*.

The third promise, "A Promise of Three Parts: Past, Present, and Future," is an overdue payment to my patient readers; namely, what happened to Brendan. My biggest surprise was how what I had thought were two drastically different story lines (Brendan's from *The Stolen* and Wraith's from *The Forgotten*) came together so perfectly. Please forgive me for taking so long to give you closure, dear readers. I hope it was worth waiting for.

The last story, "The Legion of Solomon," isn't one of the promises mentioned in the title of this collection. I had intended it to be a one-off, or perhaps lead to a series of its own someday. But the Legion of Solomon was a concept that resonated with me, and so it found its way into the American Faerie Tale universe—during the epilogue of *The Forgotten*. I'm including it—only slightly modified to fit into the AFT canon—as a thank-you, and, I hope, as a tantalizing tidbit for readers who wanted to learn more about Ovation/Collins (*The Forgotten*). I hope you enjoy learning a little more about Ovation's origin and the role the Legion plays in the mortal world.

Thanks,

Bishop O'Connell

THE LEGACY OF
PAST PROMISES

Elaine stared at the painting. While her body didn't move, her heart and mind danced in the halls of heaven. The depth and intensity of mortal passion was astounding to her, and her ability to experience it through art was like a drug. The heavy silence that filled her vast loft was broken by the high-pitched whistle of the tea-kettle. Elaine extricated herself from the old battered chair, which was so comfortable it should be considered a holy relic. She crossed her warehouse flat to the kitchen area, purposely stepping heavily so the old hardwood floor creaked. She smiled at the sound. It was like a whisper that contained all the memories the building had seen. Unlike the fae, the mortal world was constantly aging. But for those who knew how to listen, it sang of a life well lived in every tired sound. The flat took up the entire top floor of a warehouse that had been abandoned in the early 1900s. She owned it now and was its only permanent tenant. The lower floors of the five-story building were offered as a place to stay to the fifties—half-mortal, half-fae street kids, unwelcome in either world—she knew and trusted. But with all the unrest in Seattle, she was currently its only occupant.

She turned off the burner and the kettle went quiet. Three teaspoons of her personal tea blend went into the pot. The water, still bubbling, went next. The familiar and comforting aroma filled the air, black tea with whispers of orange blossom. Light poured in from the south-facing wall of floor-to-ceiling windows. But she ignored the view of the Seattle skyline. The twenty-foot ceiling was constructed of heavy wooden beams and slats, broken only by the silver of air ducts, a relatively recent addition. The floor was oak, original to the building but well maintained over the years, as were the exposed bricks of the walls and pillars. The flat was large, 5,000 square feet of open space, sparsely furnished with secondhand pieces. They had been purchased so long ago, they were technically antiques now. But she looked past all that to the paintings that covered the walls, collected over centuries and not always through strictly legal means. Nearly every school was represented by at least one piece. Her eyes followed the heavy strokes of a Van Gogh, thought lost by the general public. The emotions and impressions left behind by the artist washed over her. The melancholy and near madness, the longing and love, all mixed together like the colors of the painting itself.

The smell of her tea, now perfectly brewed, broke her reverie. As she poured tea into a large clay mug, her gaze settled on a Rossetti. Elaine smiled as she remembered seeing the painting come to life. Gabriel Rossetti—Elaine could never bring herself to think of him as Dante, it was such an absurd name—had captured Jane's beauty spectacularly. Jane Morris had been a truly beautiful mortal; it was no wonder Gabriel so often chose her as a model.

Elaine carried the mug back to her chair, sank into the plush cushions, and hit play on the remote. Vivaldi's Cello Concerto no. 4 in A Minor filled the space. She closed her eyes, letting the music fill her soul. The mournful cello danced with the playful harpsichord. She sipped her tea, opened her eyes, and her gaze fell upon another painting, the one she'd almost lost. Unwanted memories rose to the surface—and just like that, she was back in France, deep in the occupied zone.

The war—or more correctly, the Nazis—had mostly turned the once beautiful countryside and small villages to rubble. The jackbooted thugs had marched with impunity, leaving only death and destruction in their wake

Even now she could almost hear the voices of her long-dead friends.

"*Êtes-vous attentive?*"

Elaine blinked. "*Pardon?*"

François narrowed his eyes. "I asked if you were

paying attention," he said, his French heavy with a Parisian accent. "But you answer my question anyway, yes?"

There were snickers from the collection of men, scarcely more than boys, gathered around the table and map.

"Sorry," Elaine said, her own carefully applied accent fitting someone from the southern countryside. "You were saying a convoy of three German trucks will be coming down this road." She traced the route on the map with her finger. "And this being one of the few remaining bridges, they'll attempt to cross here. Did I miss something?"

François turned a little pink, then a deeper red when the chuckles turned on him. When Paul offered him the bottle of wine, François's smile returned, and he laughed as well.

"Our little sparrow misses nothing, no?" he asked, then took a swallow of wine before offering her the bottle.

Elaine smiled and accepted.

Six hours later, just before dawn, the explosives had been set and the group was in position. She sat high in a tree, her rifle held close. Despite having cast a charm to turn the iron into innocuous fae iron (a taxing process that had taken her the better part of three weeks), she still wore gloves. On more than one occasion she'd had to use another weapon, one that hadn't been magically treated.

As the first rays of dawn touched her cheeks, she had only a moment to savor the sublime joy of the morning light. Her keen eyes picked up the telltale clouds of black diesel smoke before she ever saw the vehicles. She made a sparrow call, alerting her fellow resistance fighters.

A thrush sounded back.

They were ready.

Elaine hefted her rifle and sighted down the barrel, her fingertip caressing the trigger. She watched the rise, waiting for the first truck to come into view.

Her eyes went wide and her stomach twisted when she saw the two Hanomags, armored halftrack personnel carriers, leading the three big trucks. That was two units, more than twenty soldiers. She made another birdcall, a nightingale, the signal to abort.

The thrush call came in reply, repeated twice. Proceed.

"Fools," she swore. "You're going to get us all killed."

She sighted down the rifle again and slowed her breathing. They were outnumbered almost three to one and up against armor with nothing but rifles and a few grenades.

"Just an afternoon walk along the Seine," she said. Of course Germany now controlled Paris and the Seine, so maybe it was an accurate comparison.

The caravan crawled down the muddy road, inching closer to the bridge. Looking through the scope, she watched the gunner on the lead Hanomag. His head was on a swivel, constantly looking one way then another. Not that she could blame him. This was a textbook place for an ambush.

The first Hanomag stopped just shy of the explosive charges.

Her heart began to race. Had they spotted it? No, it was buried and the mud didn't leave any sign that even she could see. No way could these mortal goose-steppers have—

An officer in the black uniform of the SS stepped out of the second Hanomag, flanked by half a dozen regular army soldiers. Elaine sighted him with her scope, noted her heartbeat, and placed her finger on the trigger.

The tingle of magic danced across her skin as the officer drew a talisman from under his coat. *"Offenbaren sich!"* he shouted.

There was a gust of wind, and the leaves on the trees near her rustled. She whispered a charm and felt it come up just as the magic reached her. The spell slid over her harmlessly. Her friends weren't so lucky. A red glow pulsed from the spot where the explosives had been set, and faint pinkish light shone from six spots around the convoy.

"Aus dem Hinterhalt überfallen!" the officer shouted and pointed to the lights.

The gunners on the Hanomags turned and the soldiers protecting the officer took aim.

"Merde," Elaine cursed, then sighted and fired.

There was a crack, and the officer's face was a red mist.

Then everything went to hell.

Soldiers poured from the trucks and the Hanomags, the gunners turned their MG-42s toward the now-fading lights marking François and the others. The soldiers took cover behind the armored vehicles and divided their fire between her and her compatriots. She was well concealed, so most of the shots did nothing more than send shredded leaves and bark through the air. Only a few smacked close enough to cause her unease.

Elaine ignored them and sighted one of the MG-42 gunners.

"*Vive la France!*" someone shouted.

Elaine looked up just in time to see Paul leap from cover and charge at the soldiers, drawing their attention and fire. She watched in horror as the Nazi guns tore him to shreds. Somehow, before falling, he lobbed two grenades into one of the armored vehicles. There came a shout of panic from inside the Hanomag and seconds later came two concussive booms. Debris flew up from the open top of the halftrack and the shouts stopped.

François and the others took advantage of Paul's sacrifice, moved to different cover, and started firing. A few Nazi soldiers dropped, but the remaining MG-42 began spraying the area with a hail of bullets.

Elaine gritted her teeth and fired two shots; both hit the gunner, and he fell. This again drew fire in her direction.

The fight became a blur after that. She took aim and fired, took aim and fired, over and over again, pausing only long enough to reload. It wasn't until she couldn't find another target that Elaine realized it was done, and all the Nazis were dead or dying.

She lay on the branch for a long moment, until the ringing in her ears began to fade. When she moved, a sharp pain in her shoulder brought her up short. More gingerly, she shifted and saw tendrils of white light filled with motes of green drifting from her shoulder. At the center was a growing blossom of gold blood. She rolled and dropped from the tree, landing only slightly less gracefully than normal. Still, the jolt made the pain jump a few numbers on the intensity scale.

She clenched her jaw, hefted her rifle, and carefully inspected the scene. The Germans were all dead, but the driver of one of the Hanomags was still alive. He took a couple shots at her with his Luger, but he'd apparently caught some ricochets or shrapnel because he didn't even come close. Elaine put him down with a shot through the viewing port.

"Please, help me," someone said in bad French.

Elaine spun to see a German soldier lying on the ground. He was little more than a kid, maybe sixteen; it didn't even look like he'd started shaving. She just stared at his tear-filled eyes, blood running down his cheek from the corner of his mouth. He had at least half a dozen holes in his chest. He was already dead, he just didn't know it.

"*Ja,*" she said.

"*Dank—*"

His thanks were swallowed by the loud report of the rifle as she put a bullet between his eyes. There was nothing she, or anyone else, could've done for him. She wiped tears away and muttered a curse at Hitler and his megalomaniacal plans.

After double-checking that all the soldiers were dead, Elaine made her sparrow call. Her mouth was so dry, the call was hardly recognizable.

Only silence answered her.

Swallowing, she hardened her heart and went to where François and the others had been taking cover. She couldn't bring herself to look down at the bloodied mess that had been Paul. She just kept walking. Her rifle fell to the ground, then she went to her knees, sobbing, covering her mouth with her good hand.

They were dead, which wasn't a surprise, but it didn't make finding them any less heartbreaking. Rémy was almost unrecognizable. If it wasn't for his blond hair, now matted with blood—Elaine's stomach twisted and she retched to one side. Michel, Julien, Daniel, Christophe, and Christian were in slightly better shape, for the most part. Julien's left arm had been chewed up by the machine gun, and Christophe's torso had been ripped open, allowing his insides to spill out. Elaine sobbed and turned to François. His rifle had been discarded and his pistol was still clutched in his left hand, two fingers having been shot off his right.

Sadness mixed with anger, and she screamed curses at him.

"You arrogant fool!" she said between sobs. "Why didn't you just call off the operation? You got them all killed!"

It wasn't long before Elaine grew numb inside. She used her fae healer's kit to remove the bullet from her shoulder, and a liberal smearing of healing ointment numbed the pain enough to give her almost full use of her arm again. Lastly, she set the pinkish, putty-like *dóú craiceann* over the wound, sealing it like a second skin. She'd never been much of a healer herself, but she got the job done. With effort, and still careful of her wounded shoulder, she dragged Paul into the cover to join his brothers-in-arms. Elaine whispered a charm and the earth drew itself up and over her friends. A moment later, lush green grass covered the seven mounds.

"Adieu, mes amis," she said softly.

She picked up her rifle and went to the trucks to see what they were carrying. The first held food supplies and ammunition. She loaded her rucksack with both, thankful she'd picked up a German Mauser and so could make use of the German ammunition. The second truck carried spare parts, likely for trucks and tanks from the look of them.

Elaine found four crates marked with the SS symbol in the last truck and searched for a means to pry them open. She came up with a tire lever and, with some effort, opened the first box, moved the packing straw away, and gasped.

Carefully, almost reverently, she withdrew the first painting from the crate. It was a Tintoretto. A fine piece, but he'd always been a tad dark for Elaine's tastes. She carefully set it aside and withdrew the second painting. Her breath caught, and she almost dropped it.

A Botticelli. She stared at herself, posed and dressed as an angel. She'd objected of course, but Sandro had been set on that idea. In the end, he'd captured her marvelously. It had been more than two hundred years since she'd seen the painting. She thought she'd never see it again.

So it was true, the Nazis were collecting artwork. Her friends would've been disappointed to find this prize. At least until she explained it would be a black eye on Hitler himself.

She checked the other crates quickly, finding more masterworks, including three Rembrandts. She packed them carefully and closed up the crates. Well aware that too much time had passed, she set the lead Hanomag free to roll forward. It set off the explosives. While the blast didn't outright destroy the Hanomag, it did ensure the vehicle wouldn't be of use to anyone coming along. Next, she collected grenades from the German soldiers and tossed a few into the back of the truck carrying spare parts. A couple more went under it, and under the lead truck as well. Both went up in a satisfying boom and began to burn. She climbed into the last truck and pushed the driver's body out. The vehicle was a poor solution, but it was the only solution. She just hoped no British or American fighter pilots flew by and decided she made an excellent target all by herself. She put the truck in gear and headed off in search of someplace to hide it. Once she could get it out of sight, she could figure out how and where to hide the paintings.

After almost an hour of incredibly tense driving, she came to a farmhouse. It was in rough shape, but the barn was intact. Luckily, the doors were large enough for the truck to fit through. She parked, killed the engine, and after a quick look around, shut the doors. After taking a moment to calm herself, she unpacked the crates and decided to hide the paintings in the hayloft. With the utmost care, she carried each up the ladder, covered it with straw, and went back for the next. When she was finished, she climbed down and examined her work from the ground level. Satisfied they were out of sight, she made her way to the farmhouse.

The door was closed but unlocked. She listened but couldn't hear anything. Rifle at the ready, she opened the door and stepped inside.

No one was there, or so it seemed.

"Bonjour?" she called out.

Silence.

"Anyone here?" she said in English.

Still nothing.

Cautiously, she made her way through the house, checking room by room to make sure it was indeed empty. Not finding anyone, she made her way to the kitchen. There, she set her rifle on the table and opened her rucksack to pull out something to eat. Luckily, she had some bread and hard cheese left, so she could save the German rations until she had no other option.

A little water was left in her canteen, and she drained it in two swallows. As she looked around to see if there was a pump inside the house, she heard movement.

She picked up her rifle and listened.

There was a faint creaking of floorboards.

Silently, she went in search of the noise. After checking every room and finding no one, she thought of the wardrobe in one of the bedrooms. No, it was too small a place to hide. She leveled her rifle at it anyway.

"Come out," she said in French. "Slowly."

She repeated the instruction in German.

"Please don't shoot us," a small voice said in German from inside the wardrobe.

It sounded like a child, and was that a Yiddish accent? Elaine almost lowered her rifle but thought better of it.

"Come out slowly," she said again in German. "I promise not to shoot."

The door opened just a little, then small fingers emerged. They gripped the door's edge and opened it very slowly.

A boy of perhaps ten stood protectively in front of a girl a few years younger. Both had yellow stars sewn to the left breasts of their jackets.

Elaine lowered her rifle.

"It's okay," she said. "I won't hurt you."

The kids looked at her skeptically.

"Are you hungry?" she asked. "I have food."

The children exchanged a glance, clearly torn between hunger and fear. She waited a moment, then turned and walked back to the kitchen. Once there, she drew out a couple of the German rations, then she heard the children coming down the hallway, trying not to make a sound. Elaine tore open the wheat crackers, then opened the canned meat. The smell wasn't appetizing to her, and she was glad to be rid of it. But then she was a vegetarian, unless she was starving.

The boy peeked around the doorway.

Elaine motioned to the table and the food, then stepped back away from it and set her rifle on the counter.

The girl rushed past her brother. She scooped meat out with a cracker and began eating. Her brother soon joined her.

Elaine forced a smile, but rage burned inside her. These were children, obviously starving. Her eyes went over the yellow stars, and she tried not to think about what had likely become of their parents. Instead, she ate the last of her bread and cheese.

"Are you a soldier?" the girl asked through a mouthful of food.

"Nessa!" the boy snapped.

"No, it's okay," Elaine said gently and smiled. "I am, sort of."

The boy eyed her rifle, then looked at her. "Have you killed a lot of Nazis?"

Elaine glanced at the rifle, then at the kids and nodded. "Some."

"The Nazis took our parents," the boy said and ate more crackers.

"You don't know that, Ezra," Nessa said.

"I do too," he said. "They told me when you were sleeping. They told me they were coming for them. Why do you think they sent us away?"

"They sent you away?" Elaine asked. The German lines were only a couple hundred kilometers from here, but she couldn't imagine how two small children, especially those marked as Jewish, could've made it across the border, let alone this far into France.

The boy nodded. "They paid a man who said he'd take us to Switzerland, and then on to America to live with our aunt and uncle."

"They live in New York," Nessa said.

Elaine forced a smile. "Where is the man who was supposed to take you?"

The two children exchanged a glance.

"He said we had to come through France, that it was safer for us than going through Germany," Ezra said.

Elaine gritted her teeth against the rising anger. Perhaps she was wrong in her assumptions. Maybe this man didn't take advantage of desperate parents and abandon two children for nothing more than money. But her experience with mortals didn't make her hopeful.

"We stopped here to rest," the boy continued. Then he shrugged. "We woke up in the morning, and he was gone. So was the cart we had been hiding in."

Fury clawed at Elaine's insides. How could anyone leave these children here? Somehow, she managed to keep outwardly calm. "How long ago was that?"

"Four days," Nessa said.

Elaine kept tears from breaking loose, but it was a near thing.

"He's not coming back, is he?" Nessa asked.

"Don't be an idiot," Ezra said. "He took Mama and Papa's money. Of course he'll come back. He promised." The boy turned to Elaine, clearly seeking confirmation from the only adult around.

Elaine fretted her lower lip. "I'm sorry," she said finally. "I don't think he's coming back."

Nessa started to cry, and Ezra wrapped his arms around her.

"I'm sorry I called you an idiot," he said softly. "Don't cry. Mama wouldn't want that."

Elaine wanted more than anything to take both of these children in her arms and hold them tight. She longed to whisper that everything would be okay, and then to somehow make it so. But she didn't move; she just looked at her boots. She noticed blood had mixed with the mud, and she couldn't help but wonder whose it was.

"Can I have some water?" Nessa asked as she wiped her eyes.

Elaine looked up. "What? Yes, of course." She drew out her canteen and turned to look for a pump, but there wasn't one.

"There is a pump outside," Ezra said, pointing the way.

"I'll go get the water," Elaine said. "You two wait here."

They nodded.

Elaine went to leave, but stopped when she heard the barn doors creak open. It was so quiet, no mortal would've heard it. She set the canteen down and turned to the kids. They might not have heard it, but they could read the expression on her face.

"Nazis?" Ezra asked in a whisper.

"I don't know," Elaine said. She reached behind her back and took out her pistol. The children tensed, but she ignore that. There wasn't time to be gentle. She handed the gun to the boy.

He took it with a shaking hand.

"Have you ever used a gun before?" Elaine asked.

The boy shook his head.

Elaine pushed his hand down so the pistol was aimed at the floor, then she took the safety off. "Keep it pointed at the ground. Don't touch the trigger unless you have to use it. Okay?"

The boy licked his lips and nodded.

"Go back to the wardrobe and wait for me there," Elaine said. "If anyone comes for you and it isn't me, you shoot them."

The boy just stared at her.

"Nessa needs you to be brave," Elaine said. "Can you do that, Ezra?"

The boy glanced at his sister, then he straightened and nodded.

"Good, now go," Elaine said. "Remember, point it at the floor unless you need to use it."

The boy nodded again, then led his sister from the

kitchen and back to the bedroom. Elaine grabbed her rifle, checked to make sure it was fully loaded, and when she heard the wardrobe door close, she went out the back door.

She crept silently around the house, keeping close to it. When she reached a corner, she peeked around to the barn.

The doors were both closed and nothing moved. Her finger tapped the trigger of her rifle and she waited. A minute later, through a hole in the barn's slats, she saw a shadow move. She reached down and picked up a stone the size of her fist, then hurled it at the barn. Before the rock struck the far corner, she had dropped to the ground and taken aim with her rifle at the barn doors.

The rock hit with a loud thud.

For a long moment, nothing happened. Then a form leapt from the window at the far end of the barn. The figure landed gracefully—too gracefully for a mortal—and rolled several times before vanishing into the tall grass.

Elaine blinked. "It can't be."

She scanned the grass looking for her target, but he was nowhere to be found. She cursed silently. Then she drew a small wooden cylinder from her pocket and held it in front of her lips.

"Who are you?" she asked in English. The magic of the cylinder carried her voice and made it sound like it was coming from inside the barn.

"Sidhe?" came a reply. The voice was definitely

male. Unfortunately, she couldn't pinpoint the source.

After a long moment, she lifted the cylinder again. "I once walked with the Dawn, and now I journey with Rogues," she said. Again her voice sounded from inside the barn.

An elf dressed in the dark green semi-military garb of a marshal stood, his hands held up. Elaine studied him. His eyes were a pale blue, almost gray, and his auburn hair just brushed the tips of his pointed ears. And he was staring right at her.

"Who are you?" she asked.

"My name is Faolan," he said.

"What do you want, Faolan?" she said.

"Could you lower the rifle?" he asked.

"I asked you first," she said.

He smiled a little and lowered his hands, but kept them away from his body. "I'm here on behalf of the Cruinnigh, looking for an elf going by the name Elaine." He waited a few heartbeats, then nodded at the rifle. "Your turn."

She debated for a long moment. There was no doubt in her head why he was here. The only surprise was that it had taken this long. Then she thought of Ezra and Nessa.

"I can't, I'm sorry," she said.

"Why?"

"Because I can't go with you. Not yet."

He looked genuinely sorry. "I'm afraid it isn't up for negotiation. I don't want to take you forcefully, but I will if I have to."

She swallowed and put her finger on the trigger. "You could try."

"Currently, you're charged only with a minor violation of the Oaths," Faolan said, unfazed. "Don't make it worse for yourself."

Elaine licked her lips, unnerved by his lack of concern. "If you could come back in a few days, that's all I need. I'll swear on my name and power to come back."

"Why? What's so important that you'd risk so much?"

She shook her head. "Considering that you're here to arrest me for involving myself in mortal affairs, I don't think you'd understand."

"Try me."

She considered for a long moment, looking him up and down. "Do you know what's happening in Germany? The industrialized murder of Jewish mortals?"

Faolan's face twisted in disgust. "Yes. And before you ask, just because the court isn't getting involved doesn't mean it's giving its consent."

"You're wrong," she said. "John Stuart Mill once said, 'Bad men need nothing more to compass their ends, than that good men should look on and do nothing.' And that's exactly what you're doing."

"We're bound by the Oaths," Faolan said. "But what does this have to do with your few days? Are you planning on going into Germany to kill Hitler?"

She shook her head. "No, nothing so grand. Though if the chance presented itself, I would." She motioned to the house with her head, never looking away from

Faolan. "In that house are two children, Jewish children. Their parents paid someone to smuggle them to safety."

He looked at the house with what appeared to be genuine concern.

"I don't know if he ran off with the money or was killed," she said. "But they're here now and alone. I want to get them to safety."

"Where were they supposed to go?"

"Switzerland, and then on to the States, New York. They have family there."

He shook his head. "They'd never get safe passage out going that way. Switzerland is neutral, but they're also not particularly compassionate to the plight of the Jewish people."

"I was going to take them to New York myself," she said. "Through the Far Trails."

He narrowed his eyes. "So you're a guide? I wasn't told that."

She shook her head. "No, I'm not. I have the means of getting them open, but—"

He laughed. "What? You're just going to wander through, looking for a pass to New York? Do you know how many paths there are through the trails?"

"It doesn't matter," she said. "I have to try. I can't just leave them here."

There was a long moment of silence as Faolan looked away and drew a slow breath.

"Okay," he said finally, turning back to her. "I'll take them."

She blinked. "You're a guide?"

He nodded. "But you'll wait here for me to return."

"No, I'm going with you," she said. "I won't let you just drop them on some corner in New York."

"You don't get a vote here," he said. "And I wouldn't do that. I know the magister of the New World Eastern Region. I'll get in touch with him and hand the children off to someone who will find their family. Then I'll come back and bring you in."

Elaine considered her options. Not having any, it didn't take long. "Thrice promised?"

"I swear the children will be safely delivered to their family," he said. "By my name, I promise that I'll see them to their family, or hand them over only to someone who likewise swears." His eyes turned hard. "I avow to deliver them safely to their family."

She lowered the rifle, got to her feet, and offered her hand. "Thank you."

He took it. "Just because we're bound not to get involved doesn't mean all of us are content with that."

Elaine nodded, a silent acknowledgment for him helping her, despite it putting him at risk. "Follow me," she said and led Faolan into the house. In the kitchen, she grabbed the canteen. "One second."

Faolan waited as she went out to the pump. After filling the canteen, she returned and went to the bedroom.

Elaine stood at the doorway, off to one side, and motioned for Faolan to do the same. "Ezra? It's me," she said in Yiddish. "It's okay. Put down the gun and come out. You and Nessa are safe, I promise."

Elaine heard the gun being set on the wardrobe's baseboard. A moment later, the door opened and the children stepped out.

"You gave a child a gun?" Faolan asked in a whisper.

"I wasn't going to leave them here defenseless if you turned out to be a Nazi patrol," Elaine said back, too low for the kids to hear.

She stepped into the room, smiled, and handed the canteen to Nessa. "Here you are, dear."

"Thank you," Nessa barely managed to say before she began sucking down the water in big gulps.

"Easy," Elaine said, lowering the girl's hands. "Drink slowly and let your brother drink when you're done."

As the kids emptied the canteen, Elaine collected the pistol and, after putting the safety on, holstered it at her back.

Nessa's eyes went wide and she drew herself in a little. "Who is that?" she asked.

Elaine turned and saw Faolan in the doorway. "He's a friend of mine," she said. "His name is Faolan." She knelt down so she was level with the kids and smiled. "He's going to take you to New York, and his friends are going to get you to your aunt. You should be with her in a couple of days."

The children stared at her in wide-eyed disbelief.

"Do you have a plane?" Ezra asked.

Faolan shook his head.

"A boat?" the boy asked.

Faolan chuckled a little. "No."

"Then how?"

Elaine smiled, then leaned in close. "It's magic, but you can't tell anyone."

The children shared a glance. Nessa was smiling and her eyes were bright. Ezra looked dubious.

"I promise," Elaine said. "This isn't a trick."

Ezra looked from Elaine to Faolan. "Is she telling the truth?"

Faolan smiled and nodded. "She is, and she's right that it's a secret. You have to promise not to tell anyone."

"I promise!" Nessa almost shouted.

Ezra blinked and looked at Elaine. "He's taking us? Does that mean you're not going?"

Elaine's smile faltered, but only a little. "No, I'm sorry."

Nessa stepped forward and threw her arms around Elaine. "Thank you for helping us," the little girl said, her face buried in Elaine's shoulder. Thankfully it was the uninjured one.

After only a moment, Ezra hugged her too.

Elaine didn't know what else to do, so she just hugged them back and kissed their cheeks. "Okay, let's get some food to take with you, then you need to get going."

Back in the kitchen, Elaine took a burlap bag from her rucksack and put some of the German rations in it, tied the end with a bit of twine, and handed it to Faolan. But Ezra reached out and took it.

"I can carry it," he said.

The elves smiled.

"Come on," Faolan said. "The best entrance is just down the road."

Elaine shouldered the rucksack and led the children out of the farmhouse, following Faolan.

Just over an hour later, they arrived at an old stone church, surprisingly intact. Faolan led them around the back where a massive oak tree stood proudly.

"You should come with us," Nessa said, taking Elaine's hand. "I'm sure our aunt would let you stay with us."

Elaine smiled and fought back tears. "I wish I could."

"Are you going to help other children?" Ezra asked. "That's it, isn't it?"

Elaine looked at the boy, then at Faolan, who seemed as interested in her answer as the boy.

"I'm going to try," Elaine said to them all. She couldn't be sure, but she thought she saw a faint smile cross Faolan's face.

"*A sheynem dank,*" Ezra said in Yiddish.

Elaine kissed the boy's forehead. "You're very welcome."

"We need to go," Faolan said. He turned to the oak, muttered a few words, and the trunk rippled then bulged as a large portal opened in the middle, filled with swirling white mist.

The children gasped, then both turned their huge eyes to Elaine.

"It's okay," she said. "Go on, your aunt is waiting."

Nessa took Ezra's hand, and they walked toward Faolan.

"I'll be back at this spot in three days," he said to Elaine.

"I'll be here," she said.

Then he ushered the children through the portal. There was a rush of power, and it closed.

Elaine stood there, looking at the tree, and let herself cry. "Do something great," she said softly.

Three days later, Elaine sat cross-legged in the ancient catacombs beneath the church, cradling her rifle in her arms in the darkness, trying to ignore the pervasive silence and the knot of anxiety that chewed at her insides. She looked over the paintings she'd moved down here for safekeeping, each propped against the stone wall so she could enjoy them. Elaine glanced over the Tintoretto painting, then she gave a final, mournful glance to the Botticelli, her Botticelli. Everyone had thought the model was Simonetta Vespucci. In truth, it had been Elaine. She knew she'd just been a stand-in, but as the passion and love Sandro had felt for Simonetta, and had put into every brushstroke, washed over her now, Elaine didn't care at all.

Elaine let out a long sigh, coming back from her memories. She wiped absently at the tears that ran down her cheeks, then took a drink of her tea. It had gone cold, but she didn't care.

Faolan had returned, and she had gone with him willingly to stand before the Cruinnigh. They charged her with violating the Oaths. Well, not technically the Oaths, just an edict of nonintervention in mortal affairs. It was really just an excuse for the nobles of the Old World Regions not to dirty their hands in the war. And Elaine had said as much.

It hadn't been a persuasive argument.

Faolan had spoken on her behalf. He tried to explain that she wasn't directly involved, but merely showing mercy for mortal children. It was no different than the court had done in the past.

Neither he, nor she, had spoken of his transgressions, how he'd violated the edict by helping her. And Elaine never would.

The regent of the Old World had retorted that these times were not like any other, that never before had so much of mortal kind been embroiled in war. The court was bound by its word not to involve itself in mortal affairs, especially not of this scale. He'd reminded Elaine that she was a noble of the Rogue Court, not some noon fae rabble, and she needed to behave as such.

It had been quite a shock to everyone, including herself, when Elaine said that if cold indifference to wholesale murder was what made a noble, she wanted no part of it.

She took another drink of her tea and smiled, remembering the look on the regent's face.

They'd stripped her of her rank and locked her

away. She shuddered, forcing down the memories of her dank cell and how the smell of exotic, blooming flowers that drifted in from the only window, far too high to see out of, almost taunted her.

She later learned from a guard that Faolan had confessed his assistance to the Cruinnigh. He was only saved from censure by the magister of the New World Eastern Region, who'd sent word that he had desperate need of Faolan's services.

It had taken almost two months of planning, and some deeds she wasn't particularly proud of, but Elaine escaped. She had been chased all over Europe by various marshals, but thankfully none had been as skilled as Faolan, so she always managed to stay one step ahead of them. When she learned that the allies had tasked a small group with saving the great works of art from Hitler, she'd helped when she could. She even handed over most of the paintings she'd found, only keeping those she was directly connected to. Her primary focus though had been on helping Jews, Gypsies, and others marked as undesirable escape the Nazi death camps; almost two hundred, mostly children, by the war's end. It was nothing compared to the millions she couldn't save, but it was something.

Eventually, after the magisters and regent could no longer deny the atrocities that had occurred, the Cruinnigh pardoned her. It was as close as they would ever come to admitting they were wrong. They did offer to restore her rank, but she refused and went to America instead.

Her eyes moved to another painting. It hung apart from the others, so it could be viewed from almost anywhere in the flat. It showed the kitchen of an old farmhouse in the northeast of France and a woman handing a tin of meat to two small children. It wasn't a masterwork, but it was more precious to Elaine than all the others put together. The artist, an elementary school teacher in New York City, and her brother, a pediatrician who was famous for not charging those too poor to pay, had fled Europe as children. Their parents had sent them away, as it turned out, mere days before being rounded up and sent to Majdanek, the less famous of Germany's labor camps.

"How many could've been saved?" Elaine asked no one, for perhaps the millionth time.

Yes, the Cruinnigh had pardoned her, but she had not, could not ever, pardon them. And now, homeless mortal children were suddenly, and unexplainably, manifesting magical powers in numbers never seen before, and changeling street kids were disappearing. All the while, the New World Western Region magister, Donovan, played the 1940s gangster boss.

Elaine picked up her cell phone and dialed.

"Well, this is a surprise," Faolan said. "It's been a while."

"Have you got a minute?" Elaine asked.

"Sure, what's wrong?"

Elaine let out a long breath. "Something bad is happening in Seattle. Someone needs to do something about it, but I think I'm in over my head."

THE PROMISE OF NEW BEGINNINGS

Edward paced the small room where he'd donned his tuxedo. It was beautifully appointed with comfortable furniture and stunning examples of plant life. He only noticed it peripherally. Fear and joy—tempered with anxiety—churned inside him as memories rose up and swallowed him like an ocean tide.

"Excuse me," Caitlin had said softly as she'd stuck her head in Edward's office door. "Dr. Huntington?"

"Yes?" Edward had said, looking up from a test result. When he saw it was Caitlin, he nearly fell out of his chair. Two weeks before, when he'd seen her for the first time, he'd been so awestruck that he'd walked right into a wall. He was still mortified. But that feeling was soon quashed by the quickening of his heart when he saw her smile. He tried not to think about how he'd altered his path through the hospital over the last two weeks so he'd see her at least a couple of times a day, mostly because it sounded creepy. Okay, even he had to admit it was a bit creepy, but he couldn't help himself.

"Do you have a moment?" Caitlin asked. She glanced around, then stepped into the office.

Edward blinked and sat up. "Oh, ah, I, um." He shook his head, which seemed to kick-start his brain, and smiled, setting the papers on his desk. "Of course, come in."

Caitlin's smile grew, and Edward fought back a sigh.

Come on, he thought, stop acting like it's high school and a cheerleader stopped to talk to you. You're not thirteen!

"Thank you," she said and closed the office door.

"What can I do for you, Ms. . . . ?" He knew what her name was, he'd overheard it while she'd been talking with some other nurses. But he suspected there was no way to let her know that and not sound exceedingly creepy.

"You can just call me Caitlin, Dr.—"

"Then you call me Edward," he said and smiled.

She pursed her lips, looked him over, then shook her head. "No, you seem more like an Eddy."

He bristled a little but found it didn't bother him as much as it usually did. Normally, he hated being called Eddy, but it didn't seem so bad coming from her. "Well, whichever you prefer."

She looked around his office and when she saw the collection of degrees, her eyebrows raised. She looked from Edward to the degrees and back again. "How—"

"I graduated high school a few years early," he said by way of explanation. He was used to the reaction. Most people his age didn't have multiple graduate degrees on top of an MD and a psychiatric certification.

Caitlin smiled bright. "You're like that old TV show from the eighties," she said, a laugh just behind her words. "*Doogie—*"

He winced.

"Shit," she said. "I'm sorry, you probably got sick of hearing that about five minutes into med school."

He smiled and felt much more at ease than he expected. "It's okay. But I don't imagine you came by to talk about child prodigies, on old sitcoms or otherwise."

Her smile faded, and now she was the one who looked uncomfortable.

"Is something wrong?" he asked.

She sighed. "How much time do you have?"

"How much do you need?" Edward answered a little too eagerly. He was about to kick himself when her genuine smile returned.

"The other nurses said you were about the nicest doctor I'd ever meet."

He blinked. "Really?" He had no idea others talked about him.

Caitlin nodded. "It's why I came by. I know you're a psychiatrist, not a therapist—"

"Actually, I do both," Edward said, again a little too quickly. "I do diagnose and treat neurological problems, but I also do psychoanalysis."

Caitlin arched an eyebrow.

"No Freud," Edward said through a laugh. "I promise." Now that he was wearing his professional hat, his confidence started to rise. "Do you think you need a therapist?"

She shrugged. "I don't really have anyone I can talk to about things. Do you see employees of the hospital?"

He nodded. "I have before, and I happen to have an opening, as luck would have it." Which was a complete lie; he was overbooked by about twenty patients, but sleep was overrated. "Why don't you have a seat, tell me why you came by, and we'll go from there. Okay?"

Caitlin nodded, then looked at the couch. "Am I supposed to lie down or sit?"

"Whatever you're comfortable with," he said, collecting a notepad and a pen. "Though most people sit."

"Thank God," she said and perched on the edge of the leather sofa.

"You can use the whole cushion," he said.

Caitlin laughed and moved back, sitting more comfortably. Eddy moved to the leather chair and sat down.

"So how does this work?" Caitlin asked. "Do I just start talking?"

"Pretty much," Edward said. "We can talk about whatever you like. You can tell me as much or as little as you're comfortable with, but the more you tell me, the easier it is for me to help."

Caitlin closed her eyes, drew in a deep breath, and let it out slowly. "Okay, you asked for it."

In the end, he'd concluded that she didn't need a

therapist, just someone to listen, and he'd told her as much. Though he promised himself—and her after they'd become friends—that if he ever thought she did need professional help, he'd refer her immediately to someone else.

Edward smiled as he thought back to that first visit. It had lasted more than two hours and had ended only then because she'd had to get to a parenting class. It still made his heart full to think of how much she'd opened up to him right away. She'd told him in that first visit about losing her parents as a child. She'd even told him about James and finding out she was pregnant while still grieving the loss of the grandparents who'd raised her. Even then he'd admired her strength and courage. She'd seen so much loss in her life, but she still was able to give comfort to patients for twelve hours and make it look easy.

Then he started to think about when Fiona had been taken—five years later—and how his and Caitlin's relationship had evolved, rather quickly, after that. He loved her and had for years. While he didn't doubt she loved him, he couldn't help but wonder if maybe her feelings had been helped along by the traumatic events of the last year: the kidnapping and rescue, and everything that happened around that. Who was to say that any day she wouldn't come to her senses, grab Fiona, and head for the hills? Who was to say that day wasn't today? He had plenty of confidence when it came to his profession and his intelligence, but he knew he was far from a catch. He was a thirty-two-year-old virgin—

"Relax, it's going to fine," Dante said.

"What?" Edward stopped midstride and turned to face Dante. The elf was sitting on the arm of a plush chair, looking incredibly suave in his tailored tuxedo. His blond hair, which had been shoulder length for as long as Edward had known him, was now cut short and perfectly styled. Edward felt an inferiority complex start to overcome him. Then he remembered it was Dante, and that James Bond would feel inferior. That thought helped, a little.

"What the man is saying," Henry said, his voice carrying a soft Southern drawl, "is that you're going to wear a hole in his floor if you keep pacing like that."

Edward turned to his best man, his friend and former roommate from medical school. Henry was taller than Edward, though still several inches shorter than Dante. He sat in another chair, giving Edward a calm, casual smile that embodied Southern charm.

"Today isn't about you; it's about Caitlin," Dante said.

"He's right," Henry said and smiled. "Trust me, soon as you see her walk down that aisle, looking every bit like an angel stepped from heaven, with eyes only for you, nothing else in the world will matter. In fact, you'll probably need a little prompting to remember your own name."

"I don't recall you being this nervous when you married Hannah," Edward said.

"No, I wasn't the least bit nervous," Henry said and shrugged. "Black man marrying a white woman in Louisiana—whatever could I have been nervous about?"

Edward winced and muttered something under his breath. "I'm sorry, I didn't think about that, I just—"

"I always liked that about you," Henry said.

"My ability to deftly slip my foot into my mouth?" Edward asked.

"That is a rather remarkable talent," Dante said.

"It is at that," Henry said and chuckled. "But to my original point, if you think I gave one moment of worry to what anyone else thought, you're a fool." He shook his head. "I had no room for those thoughts. I just kept picturing Hannah coming to her senses and making a run for it, or me passing out halfway through the ceremony." He laughed again. "Or that old preacher falling over dead—"

Now Edward burst into laughter. "That's right! I forgot about him. Dear lord, how old was he?"

"Ninety-seven," Henry said. "Momma wanted him to marry me and Hannah like he married her and Daddy." Henry shook his head. "I think he might've married Moses and Zipporah."

Edward's laughter faded when he looked at Dante. The elf's smile had softened and become a little bittersweet. Edward realized then that he didn't know anything about Dante's romantic past. Had he ever been married? Had he loved someone but was never given the opportunity to pursue it? His hand was in his pocket, obviously worrying at something. Edward thought he recognized the look on Dante's face and wondered if the regent was thinking not of a past love but of a lost friend. The elf was still the same to anyone who didn't know what to look for, but since Brendan's memorial, something in Dante had changed. How could it not? They'd memorialized a man no one was sure was even dead. It was one of those things you knew everyone was thinking about because no one ever said anything about it. Edward wondered if Dante's dramatic haircut, going from shoulder length to close cropped, was a coping mechanism.

Edward drew in a deep breath and exhaled. Then he thought of how lucky he was. He was living with the woman he loved and her beautiful daughter, even if he'd been unsure about the prospect when Caitlin had presented it. He couldn't help but smile to remember the conversation.

"I can't sleep," Caitlin had said. "I'm a zombie at work, and it's starting to affect Fiona. I've got four deadbolts on every door, alarms on the windows, and I sleep with a gun under my pillow." She shook her head. "I'm tired, Eddy, and I'm tired of being afraid."

He remembered how she'd looked at him then. There was no desperation or fear in her eyes. In fact, she had smiled, and that had taken him aback.

"It's not a home anymore," she said. "Fergus and the oíche took that from me. Maybe it could be again someday, but I don't want it to be."

He'd tried to speak, but she'd just placed her fingertips over his lips.

"I want to make a new home." She stepped closer. "I

want that home to be with you, but if you're not ready for that, I understand. There are some apartments I've found that I think would work." She kissed him then, very softly. "But I'll need help moving my sofa, and it's really heavy."

He smiled back. "Well, I'm not moving a sofa, so you'll just have to move in."

She had pulled the ring from her pocket then and held it out to him. He'd stared at it for a long time like an idiot, his brain not registering what he was seeing.

"But I'm not just going to move in with some guy," she said. "Will you marry me?"

"I, uh, um."

She touched her fingers to his lips again and looked at him unblinking. "I've been thinking about this for a while now. I'm not asking you because of what happened, because I'm afraid, or because I don't want to be alone. I'm asking because I love you, because I want to grow old with you, and I can't think of anyone who will be a better father to Fiona."

"Yes," was all he'd been able to say before he couldn't keep from kissing her any longer.

Now that woman was going to marry him. There had been enough pain, grief, and loss for everyone. It was time for some joy.

Edward stepped over to Dante and held out his hand. "Thank you for being here," he said, "And for walking Caitlin down the aisle." And for everything else, he added silently.

Dante looked at his hand, then into Edward's

eyes. In that brief moment, they said volumes to each other. Dante's smile returned; a genuine smile, if only for a moment. He stood, took the offered hand, then wrapped his other arm around Edward.

"It means a great deal you've let me be a part of your lives," Dante said.

"It's like Caitlin said, you're family." Edward stepped back. "And after today, that makes you my family too."

"And yet you chose me for your best man?" Henry said.

Edward smiled and shrugged. "Pity and obligation."

Henry feigned a wince. "Oh, you do cut me, sir."

There was a knock at the door, and the nervousness Edward had briefly forgotten returned with a vengeance.

Dante opened the door, allowing Edward's groomsmen, Hiro and Thomas, into the makeshift bridegroom's room, a private room off the main dance floor of Dante's club. Despite looking barely old enough to drink—Hiro was actually almost forty—he was one of the best pediatric oncologists in the country.

Thomas was the president of the hospital where Edward, Caitlin, and Hiro worked. The tailored lines of his tux complemented his athletic build and the stylish lines of gray at his temples. Sure, some could say it was odd to ask your boss to be a groomsman, but Edward had never had a lot of friends, and fewer still outside work. In fact, if you didn't count Henry, he had no friends outside of work.

"It's almost time," Thomas said. "Everyone's here."

Edward tried to slow his breathing, but his heart was racing. It was really happening.

"I think that's my cue," Dante said. He patted Edward's shoulder.

"You'll make sure she doesn't back out, right?" Edward asked.

"No promises."

Edward laughed nervously, then gave Dante a flat look. "No, seriously."

Dante laughed. "She made me promise the same thing about you."

"Really?" Edward asked.

Dante winked. "Don't keep her waiting."

"Relax." Hiro shrugged and flashed his infectious smile. "It's only for the rest of your life."

"Only if I'm lucky," Edward said.

"You're one of the last true romantics, Dr. Huntington," Thomas said.

Edward smiled, but it was short-lived when he heard a familiar voice in the hallway.

"Yes, I know it's about to begin," Edward's mother said. "But I'm going to see my son."

Edward winced. It wasn't that his mother was mean, or cruel, she'd just been born without any tact, or much empathy.

"You should probably go," Edward said to his groomsmen. "I'd prefer if you weren't here for this."

The three men exchanged a glance and then made their exit.

Edward's mother and father rounded the corner as

Hiro, Henry, and Thomas stepped out of the room. There was a moment of awkward dancing as everyone tried to shuffle past each other in the narrow hallway. Edward's father, who looked just like Edward but with more years and gray hairs, gave a polite nod. His mother, a short and slender woman with severe features and expertly dyed dark brown hair, bowled past them as if they didn't exist.

"Mother, what are you doing?" Edward asked when she stepped up to him. "The wedding is going to start—"

"I'm well aware of that, Edward," she said.

He felt like he was six years old again.

"Are you sure this is what you want?" She asked it in a tone more fitting to a mother being told by her six-year-old that he wants to join the circus.

"What?" Edward asked, a little louder than he intended.

His mother shook her head, let out an exasperated sigh, then turned to Edward's father. "Daniel, a little help please."

Edward's father smiled and nodded. "Of course." He looked at Edward, then around the hall they stood in.

"Yeah," Edward said. "You should probably come in here."

"Yes, not yeah," his mother said.

He stepped back, and his parents came inside, his mother closing the door behind them. Edward swallowed back his rising dread. It wasn't that he didn't love his parents, he did. They just were never a very close or loving family. His father was a professor of pure mathematics at MIT, and his mother was a lawyer focused on patent and international law. They were analytical, logical people, not given to affection or intimacy. It was a bit like being raised by Vulcans.

And yet I turned out so normal, Edward thought. A wizard psychiatrist.

His whole life had been one long attempt to earn his parent's approval. He knew his mother didn't approve of Caitlin, or any single mother. He'd known this conversation was coming for months, but he'd been avoiding it. There was no way around it now, and Caitlin deserved better from him.

He went to the wet bar and poured two fingers of whiskey. He didn't bother offering his parents any, they didn't drink. He emptied the glass in one long gulp, then set it down and steeled his will before turning around.

"Fine, Mother," he said. "Let's have this conversation. You were asking me, on my wedding day no less, if I want to marry the woman I love."

His mother let out an exasperated sigh. "Good lord, don't be so dramatic."

"What she's asking," his father said, "is if you've really thought this through."

"No, that isn't what she's asking," Edward said. "Not really."

"I like Caitlin," his mother said.

Edward opened his mouth to call out the lie, but his mother just kept talking.

"We both do," she said. "She's a very nice girl—"

"Woman," Edward corrected, not bothering to keep the heat from his tone. "She's not a child, she's a grown woman."

"Fine," Edward's mother said. "But you aren't just marrying her. There's also Fiona."

Edward drew in a slow breath.

"She's a delightful child," his father said.

"But she isn't yours," his mother said. "Are you prepared to raise another man's child?"

Edward opened his mouth.

His mother waved a hand dismissively. "This isn't about her being a single mother, or the real father not being around," his mother said in a tone that suggested it was precisely about that. "It's about—"

"Stop," Edward said, slamming the glass down onto the counter so hard he was surprised it didn't shatter.

Both his parents stared at him speechless.

"Let me put both your minds at ease." He looked from his mother to his father and back. "Caitlin is the kindest, strongest, bravest person I've ever known. She's raising a child on her own. She doesn't ask for pity or sympathy from anyone because of the life she's had. What she does do is face things head on that would make most people run screaming. She's kind and comforting to people who are in pain and scared. She's not just a good person, she's remarkable. She's been nothing but kind to you whenever you've met her, and the best you could do is barely hidden disdain. I won't have it anymore. I love her, I have since we first met."

His mother opened her mouth, but he ignored her, the catharsis of the moment urging him on.

"If you can't see what an astounding woman Caitlin is," Edward said, "then I can only feel pity for you. Now, you're right that Fiona isn't my biological daughter, but I couldn't love her more if she was. My only regret is that I didn't have a role in making her. But I consider myself incredibly lucky. Her mother is willing to let me play a role in raising her, and I'll get to see her grow into a remarkable woman."

"Edward—" his mother said.

"I'm sorry, I forgot to answer your question. Yes," Edward said with the conviction and certainly he felt in his soul, and he realized then that all his doubts and worries were gone. "I know what I'm 'getting into.' Yes, I've thought about it. Yes, I know what it means. This is what I want. And I've never been as certain of anything in my life as I am of that."

There was a long, awkward silence and Edward began to feel the faintest twinge of remorse.

"I'm sorry if my words and tone are harsh," he said, his tone just a bit softer. "But this is quite possibly the rudest, most inappropriate thing anyone could do today."

His mother flushed red and glanced away.

"Now, if you'll excuse me, I'm off to marry the woman I love," Edward said, moving to the door. "If you can show us both some common courtesy and respect, you're welcome to stay. If not, please see yourselves out."

He stepped out and closed the door behind him.

Henry was waiting in the hallway.

Edward cleared his throat and tried to look relaxed. "Hey, um—"

Henry nodded. "I heard it all."

"Oh."

"Just let it go, you've got other things to focus on today."

Edward nodded and started walking, Henry taking up step beside him.

"Just look on the bright side," Henry said.

"Which is?"

"At least they didn't wait for the preacher to ask if anyone objected."

There was a brief moment of silence before both of them started laughing and made their way to Edward's future.

Caitlin smiled as she watched Fiona play with her stuffed Paddy Bear. The little girl's dress was a miniature of her mother's, except it had shoulder straps instead of off-the-shoulder three-quarter sleeves. Paddy Bear, for his part, was sporting a white bowtie that Dante had procured just for this occasion. As her friends chatted and smiled, Caitlin smiled. Up until very recently, she'd quietly given up on the idea of ever having a wedding or a family, beyond Fiona anyway. It was never an overt, conscious decision, it was just that between her job and Fiona, meeting anyone—much less building a relationship—wasn't high on her list of priorities. But Eddy had found his way into her heart anyway. And now here she was, dressed in a beautiful gown, waiting to marry the man she loved. She laughed quietly to herself, remembering the look on Eddy's face when she'd pulled out the ring. That was a memory she was going to hold on to for the rest of her life.

At the edges of her mind, a voice whispered, reminding her of other memories. And when Fiona looked up at her with big green eyes, Caitlin thought of another pair of green eyes. She saw the brownie's agonized, child-like face as the gangrene-like blackness spread across its little body. She still could hear its sobs, and it tore her soul apart all over again.

Caitlin knew there'd been no choice at the time, not if she was going to rescue Fiona from Fergus and his band of nightmares. But the reason there had been no choice was because she'd fallen right into the trap the oíche had set. She'd ignored Brendan's advice.

She drew in a long breath, pushing the pain down deep. She'd gotten good at this part. At first it had just been nightmares, but as the wedding drew closer, the dying cries of the innocent faerie haunted her days more and more often. She'd told Eddy about them, and all her feelings of guilt and shame. He'd reacted exactly as she knew he would. He'd told her, repeatedly, that it wasn't her fault. The oíche had killed the brownie; they'd just used Caitlin to do it. That she was a good person, and had done what she had to do. Survivor's guilt, he called it. She knew he was right, but in her heart, it didn't help much, or for long.

Then there was Brendan's sacrifice. Eddy said Brendan had made his choice and she should respect it. Again, she knew he was right, but that didn't make it, or any of the rest, easier to live with. It was made all the harder because she knew everyone wondered if Brendan had actually died. No one ever said it aloud, but she knew it. She also knew the unspoken question that followed: What fate befell him if he hadn't died?

After all she'd done, did she still deserve this day? She thought of how Eddy looked at her, all the love she could see in his eyes. He'd been beyond amazing this past year. She remembered that first night after she and Fiona had moved into his house, which was also the first night together after she'd asked him to marry her. When she'd first come to his bed, making it their bed, and told him she just wanted him to hold her, he hadn't argued, or even said a word. He'd just wrapped her in his arms and held her all night, and every night after. He'd never pushed for more, never even brought it up. She knew he was waiting for her to make the first move, and she both hated and loved that he hadn't tried anything. Could she blame him though? He knew she'd committed murder.

"You should be happy," Kris said as she rubbed Caitlin's shoulder.

Caitlin was grateful her maid of honor, like Fiona, didn't seem to remember anything from that horrible couple of days. Casey and Janet, her bridesmaids, stepped over.

Casey pushed a mimosa into Caitlin's hand. "You look like you could use a drink."

Caitlin accepted the glass and took a sip, even though she didn't want it. "Thanks." She smiled, glad to find it genuine.

"It's normal to have second thoughts," Kris said, squeezing Caitlin's hand.

"Especially considering the in-laws," Janet said and laughed.

Caitlin shook her head. "I'm not, not really. I'm just thinking about things." Of course she worried about Eddy coming to his senses and running for the hills, but not really. Through all her wallowing and self-loathing, the one thing she never doubted, not really, was that he loved her. Now, whether she deserved that love, or him, was a different question.

"He loves you," Casey said. "And you love him, even if it did take you a while to figure that out."

Caitlin nodded and let those words soak in. She did love Eddy, with all her heart. There had been a period after Fiona was safely home that she'd wrestled with her feelings for him. In fact, she'd spent several nights, unable to sleep in a house where she didn't feel safe, doing some in-depth soul searching on it. Then some months later, after he'd come over for dinner, and Caitlin had actually managed to get a couple hours sleep— she always did after he'd come over—she'd found herself wishing he was there, that he'd stayed. Not out of any sense of fear, or insecurity, but simply because she wanted to hold him and kiss him, to just enjoy having him close. That day she'd used her lunch break to find the ring. And then, that first night together, Eddy had wrapped her in his arms. In that moment, she knew she wanted nothing more than to hold him back, to kiss him, and to shower him with love for the rest of her life.

Then do it, moron, she told herself. *Stop feeling sorry for yourself. End the goddamned pity party and start living your life!*

She smiled as she thought of that, of the years ahead of them, of growing old together and watching Fiona become a woman.

That's exactly what I'm going to do, she told herself. She might've done the best she could, but ultimately they'd been terrible choices, and carried horrible consequences. However, that didn't mean she couldn't make it all mean something.

In that moment, with that decision, it felt as if she'd set aside a heavy load. She drew in a deep breath, and felt herself sit up straighter. She smiled, and it was born from not just happiness but hope.

"That's more like it," Janet said and drank from her own mimosa. "Besides, if you let him go, I'm going after him."

Everyone laughed.

There was a knock at the door, and it opened a crack.

"Are you ladies decent?" Dante asked without stepping in.

"No, but we're dressed," Casey said. "Damn it all," she added under her breath.

There was more laughter, though quieter.

Dante stepped in, and Caitlin shook her head as Kris and Casey swooned a little. Not that she could blame them. He was tall, charming, and absolutely beautiful. Caitlin smiled more as it dawned on her that even as good as Dante looked in his tux, she thought of Eddy.

When Caitlin came back to herself, she found Dante staring at her.

"What?" she asked, suddenly nervous. "Do I look okay?"

Dante leaned in and kissed her forehead. "You look radiant, an absolute vision."

Her friends sighed.

Caitlin felt her face flush.

"I hope Edward remembers how to talk when he sees you," Dante said.

Caitlin turned away, sure her cheeks were a bright pink, but she smiled and thought of how cute, and so very Eddy, it would be if that happened.

"And you," Dante said, turned, and kneeled in front of Fiona, "look just like your mommy, and just as beautiful."

Fiona smiled and gripped Paddy Bear in a hug. "Thank you, Dante." The little girl leaned forward and kissed Dante's cheek.

"Oh, lucky me," he said and winked at her. "You're going to save a dance for me, right?"

"Aw," Janet, Kris, and Casey said in unison.

Dante stood and turned to Caitlin. "Are you ready?"

She opened her mouth, unsure of what was about to come out.

Dante took her hands in his and just stared at them. "You both deserve this." When he spoke, his voice was so low Caitlin had to strain to hear him. "We all have darkness in our past. It's what we do with it that makes us who we are."

Caitlin felt shame and guilt try to rise up in her, but she didn't give them any power this time. Instead, she squeezed Dante's hands and smiled. "I'm ready."

As if on cue, Canon in D Major began to play outside.

There was a flurry of movement around Caitlin, and she felt a bit like she was standing in the eye of a hurricane. The bridesmaids adjusted dresses and checked each other's hair. Someone pushed Caitlin's bouquet into her hand. Someone else handed Fiona the basket of coral-colored rose petals. She promptly set Paddy Bear in it and was led to the front of the line by Casey.

"Thank you," Caitlin whispered as she slipped her arm through Dante's.

Dante squeezed her hand. "It's truly my honor and privilege to walk you down the aisle."

"No, I don't just mean that," she said.

"I know," Dante said. "That's my honor and privilege as well."

Then they were walking out the door. The fresh,

heady smell of the trees and flowers that filled Dante's club washed over Caitlin. She was amazed how completely the place had been transformed. Everywhere she looked there were bright flowers, ivy, or silk fabric hangings in her wedding colors. It was hard to believe this was the main floor in one of the most popular night spots in Boston.

Everyone stood and smiled as Fiona made her way down the aisle, casting rose petals out in front of her, pausing every couple of steps to pick up Paddy Bear and set him back in the basket.

Caitlin laughed then tried not to look at the guests who rose for her procession. She had no one really, save those in her wedding party; and while Eddy's family wasn't large, he did have one. In fact, they'd spent hours scrounging their past, only to fill a third of the forty seats. When she saw the bride's section nearly full, she almost tripped. As she looked from one smiling face to another, she saw they were all fae. Some were elves, all of those who had helped Dante and Eddy stop the wizard, but there were countless others. Almost every kind of fae was represented, and they were all looking at her with serene smiles. Except for Faolan. He beamed at her and winked.

Caitlin's gaze went to Eddy's parents. His father smiled, but his mother didn't look her way—she was watching Fiona. Caitlin almost thought she saw the faintest trace of a smile. If anyone could bring Eddy's mother around, and make the family come together, it would be Fiona.

"A wizard has nothing on the power of a little girl," she whispered, too low for anyone to hear over the music. Or so she thought, until she saw Dante's slight smile.

All this happened within the first five steps. On the sixth, she drew in a breath, looked up, and saw Eddy. The rest of the world vanished. He looked at her like no one ever had. His eyes were a little wide and his mouth hung open. It was clear that she was, to him at least, the most beautiful thing he'd ever seen. For his part, he looked incredibly handsome in his tuxedo; his eyes were shining and his crooked smile tugged at her heart, which felt like it might burst. In that moment, every doubt, every fear, every bit of guilt vanished.

Dante led her to Edward and then placed her hand in his, kissed Caitlin's cheek, and took his seat next to Faolan.

She hardly heard anything the minister, an elf named Riley, said, and apparently Edward didn't either.

The minister cleared his throat and whispered to Edward, "You're on."

"Sorry, I was, ah, a little distracted," Edward said.

There was a rustle of faint laughter from the guests.

Edward drew a breath and looked at Caitlin in a way that made her heart start to melt.

"Caitlin," he began, "I've loved you from the first moment I saw you." He smiled. "Literally. Though I think you might've picked up on that, since I walked into a wall."

More laughter.

"You came to me looking for help, for a friendly ear, but something incredible happened instead," he said. "You became my best friend. You let me into your life, trusting me with what you held most precious." He smiled at Fiona. "We might not have had the most traditional start to our relationship—"

Dante and Faolan chuckled softly.

"—and I don't know what the future holds for either of us," Edward continued. "But I can promise that I will love you, and Fiona, for the rest of my life. I will count each day that I get to love you as a gift. I know I'll screw up." He smiled. "I sort of excel at that."

Caitlin wiped at the tears on her cheeks and laughed.

"But I'll love you, both of you. I love you now, and I will forever and always." Caitlin drew in a breath and swallowed back more tears as he slipped the ring on her finger, a white gold band and diamond encircled by a yellow gold Celtic knot design. "You are truly the love of my life. And however much I have, I give it to you."

There was a moment of silence. Caitlin blinked, then realized it was her turn.

"Eddy," she said, "you loved me from the start with the kind of unconditional, selfless love I didn't believe existed. You were always there for me when I needed you most." She squeezed his hand tight. "Never hesitating, never questioning. You were my best friend long before I was yours. I wish I'd seen sooner what was right in front of me, that I loved you. You are a gift, and I promise to love you for all my days. I will make sure there is never a day when you don't know how much you mean to me. I love you, Eddy, now, forever, and always."

Kris handed her the ring, and Caitlin slipped it on Eddy's finger. It was a match to Caitlin's, save with no diamond.

"By the power vested in me, I now pronounce you husband and wife," the minister said. "You may kiss—"

Caitlin threw her arms around Edward, practically tackling him, and kissed him, losing herself in the softness of his lips and the feel of his arms around her. After a moment, he kissed her back, and in that moment, there was no darkness, no sadness, no guilt or shame. There was only hope, love, joy, and light. She knew there would be troubles, but it was time to leave the past behind. This was a new beginning, for them both.

As the kiss drew to a close, a small voice broke through the applause and cheers.

"Is he my daddy now?" Fiona asked.

Edward didn't answer, he just nodded.

Caitlin kissed the tears from his eyes.

"I love you," he whispered. "Both of you."

"And we love you too," she whispered.

"Ladies and gentlemen," the minister said as they turned to face the guests. "It is my pleasure to introduce for the first time, Dr. Edward Huntington, and Mrs. Caitlin Brady-Huntington."

A PROMISE OF THREE PARTS: PAST, PRESENT, AND FUTURE

Brendan thought back, trying to remember what had come before. Time had no meaning here, which made the memories—if they were in fact memories—hard to place in the right order.

"Do you want to remember, love?" Áine asked, her cheek to his chest. There was sadness in her tone.

"I don't know," Brendan said, wrapping his arms around her and drawing her closer. "Not if it means leaving this place and losing you again." He had lost her before, hadn't he? He flinched at a flash of memory, of Áine dying in his arms, covered in blood from wounds she suffered at his hands. "No!"

"Shh, *A rún mo chroí*," Áine whispered and held him tighter. "It's okay. It weren't you."

Brendan knew that was true, it'd been the demon inside him, the spirit of rage. But he'd been the one to lose control of it.

"You did good things as well," she said. "Do you remember those? If you remember, you must remember it all."

He hesitated, unsure if he wanted to. When he looked into Áine's shining eyes, the memories slowly rose up from the darkness. "I remember you, Áine—no, not you, what was her name, then?"

"Caitlin, love," Áine said softly.

Brendan nodded. "Aye, Caitlin, that's it." He shook his head. "She was the very image of you."

Áine smiled. "Aye, I know. She would be, wouldn't she?"

"Her daughter had been taken by the oíche," Brendan said. "I remember working with Dante to find where they'd taken her." The memories slowly unfolded, one leading to another. "She and I, the two of us, we went to the Tír to get Fiona, the *girseach*, back from Fergus." Brendan stopped. He could sense something dark and terrible just ahead.

Áine moved up and kissed his brow. "It's okay, my beloved, keep going."

Brendan drew her closer, as if the memories might tear Áine from him. "I remember the Dusk Lands, the three challenges, and a promise—"

"Aye, that's right," Áine said. "You promised to get Caitlin and Fiona out." She buried her face in his neck. "And you did just that."

It was all blood and fury now, and it was good. Brendan closed his eyes. "Bloody hell, I gave in to the thing, didn't I? Loosed the monster once and for all?"

Áine nodded, reaching up to brush a tear from his eye. "It was the only way. And you gave all to keep your promise."

It was like falling for a moment, and Brendan reached out, desperate hands grasping for Áine, but only finding empty air. And then he was back in the heart of the Dusk Lands, where the Dark King was his most powerful. Fergus had told them of his plan to make Fiona—his own daughter—his queen. With her shaped by him, and the Dawn Court blood she inherited from her mother, Fergus would cast out Queen Teagan and take the Dawn Court for himself. But Brendan had been wounded and, bound by Fergus, helpless to do anything.

"There is another option." Fergus reached out with his free hand and caressed Caitlin's face. "You needn't lose our child."

She winced at his touch, but didn't pull away.

Brendan could smell the magic pouring off Fergus and drifting around Caitlin.

"Stay here, with Fiona," he said, his voice like warm silk.

"What?"

"Think of it. Fiona will be safe." He said. "She'll never get sick, never grow old, and neither will you. She will be a queen, wanting for nothing. Think what a life that will be for her."

Brendan felt a rush of panic. Don't let him trick you! he shouted, but nothing came out. All the while, he struggled to reach the knives at his back. If he could just get to his blades, his steel blades, he could do something. He looked to the oíche, every one of them wearing a smug smile. One even licked his lips. Brendan's hand moved a hair closer to his knife, and would go no closer. He swore silently and kept trying, but it was no use. The knife was less than six inches away, but it might as well be a thousand miles.

"All need not be lost," Fergus said. "I'll set the Fian free if you stay. No others need die."

Caitlin looked at Brendan.

He looked at her, his eyes begging her not to do it.

Fergus leaned in close and whispered something into her ear that Brendan couldn't hear. Caitlin drew in a breath and looked at Fiona. She smiled briefly before her eyes drifted over the court. Then her eyes closed and tears spilled down her cheeks. She wiped them away, reached into a pocket, and pulled out Fiona's stuffed bear. When she opened her eyes, she looked right at Brendan.

"I'm sorry, Brendan," she said. "I have to." Brendan knew just what she was doing, and from Fergus's reaction, it was working.

Fergus smiled wide and held his hand out to Caitlin. "Come, my dear."

Caitlin swallowed and stepped forward, taking Fergus's hand.

He drew her into his arms and whispered into her ear again.

Brendan closed his eyes and knew what he had to do. Not the girl or her mother, he said silently to the demon of rage inside him. There are plenty of others for you! But not the mother or her child.

There was a silence, as if the monster was considering it. *Very well. As you wish,* it finally said.

I'll have your oath, then!

I swear it by my name and my power! the monster said, clearly eager for death and blood.

As Brendan opened his eyes and readied himself, a sudden realization came to him. He was at the center of Fergus's power, preparing to face down the faerie king of the Dusk Court. Was this what his parents had in mind when they'd bound this spirit of rage to him? No one, not even Fionn and the first Fianna, would've been able to stand against Fergus. Did they bind this monster to him so that one day, if he had to, he could?

The demon didn't answer, but maybe it didn't have to.

Brendan watched Caitlin as she stepped close to Fergus. Brendan smiled when he saw her hand move to her back and slip under her jacket. Fergus was too busy basking in his victory. He never saw her draw the blade. He had no idea what was happening until Caitlin buried the steel into his back.

Fergus pushed her away as she yanked it out and stumbled, more out of surprise than injury. Caitlin slashed out. Fergus grunted in pain as the blade cut across his right hand. It came open on reflex, and the purple crystal he'd been holding so close fell to the ground.

Brendan saw all the oíche's eyes go wide and their mouths turn up into grins. Fergus tried to catch the crystal, but he missed and it struck the tiles, causing a piece to break off.

"No!" Fergus roared, nearly shaking the standing stones around them. "You insufferable, mortal *striapach!*" He backhanded Caitlin, then picked up the crystal and broken shard.

Caitlin landed on the hard stone a step away from Brendan.

The silver cords began to flicker as Fergus's attention and power slipped.

Fergus rounded on Caitlin, but Brendan could see he didn't have the same power he had moments before.

"I'll show you pain and torment you never dreamed were possible," Fergus said.

"No," Caitlin said, wiping blood from her lip. "You made a promise. You swore to me. Don't you remember?"

Aye, love, Brendan answered silently. I remember, and I mean to keep it.

Fergus, the arrogant fool, narrowed his brow. "I made no promise."

Caitlin blinked her wet eyes, and the last of her tears escaped. "You promised me and you promised her. I need you to keep it now."

The ocean of rage inside Brendan burst into flames, and it was so vast, so complete, the devil himself would've cowered from it. Brendan's soul sang in delight.

Fergus's eyes went wide in realization, and he turned to Brendan.

"Brendan," Caitlin said through a sob, "you promised to save my little girl!"

Aye, Brendan said without a word. And I'll make them all pay for what they did to you, and to Áine.

And now death has come for the immortal fae! the monster sang.

Fergus took a step back.

Strength like Brendan had never known poured into him. There was a loud crack as the silver cords snapped and vanished.

"*TAR AMACH, A BHÁIS!*" Brendan roared. Pain, injury, all of it became meaningless. There was only rage, only battle, only blood and death. His eyes met Fergus's as claws emerged from his hands.

"*FÁG AN BEALACH!*" Brendan screamed, drew his knives, and hurled them. They streaked through the air, little more than a blur, and hit two oíche so hard they were lifted clear off the ground. Clouds of darkness and sparks trailed them as they flew back behind the throne and vanished.

Brendan saw Caitlin roll to her feet, grab her knife, and sprint toward Fiona.

Fergus turned to follow, but Brendan leapt on him, driving the fae king to the ground.

As his claws dug into Fergus's sides, he bent low and whispered into his ear, "I am the end of you and your court."

Fergus grabbed Brendan's arm and tossed him across the courtyard, but Brendan landed on his feet.

"DÍOLTAS!" he yelled. His knives leapt into the air, and into his hands. A banshee opened its mouth to wail, but Brendan drove his knife in, and the banshee near exploded in a cloud of darkness and red lights. Others moved in, but Brendan turned to find Fergus. Brendan saw him reach out for Caitlin as she reached for Fiona. He grabbed Caitlin's shoulder, but she spun and drove her knife into his shoulder, burying it to the hilt.

Fergus screamed and let her go.

Leaving the blade, Caitlin grabbed Fiona, pushed the bear into her little hands, and turned. Fergus grabbed for her, but Brendan leapt, throwing his knives as he did, destroying another banshee and a dusk elf. He landed on Fergus, claws sinking into flesh, and hurled the Dark King across the courtyard and into the frantic mob.

Brendan turned to Caitlin and took a step forward. They could go, all of them. He could see them both safely out!

But Caitlin's reaction chilled him to his soul. She just stared at him with absolute fear in her eyes. She turned her body, shielding Fiona. "Brendan, remember!"

Shame pushed its way up through the fury and rage. He knew then, there was no going back. Not for him. Not ever.

You're a monster, remember. There is no place for monsters in the quiet village. But it takes a monster to destroy monsters!

"Please, remember," she said again.

He clenched his fists and wanted to say, to scream, that he never forgot, that he never would. But he couldn't. He looked from Caitlin to Fiona and thought of Áine, wondered what might've been for his child and her mother.

We have a bargain, the demon said. *You have a promise to keep to me as well, monster.*

"Go," Brendan said to Caitlin, so softly even he couldn't hear it. "GO!" he screamed this time, then he turned and leapt onto an oíche who was trying to escape, calling his knives back to him. He cut the oíche down with one blade, a dusk elf with the other. Through the darkness and twinkling lights that danced around him, Brendan saw Caitlin and Fiona vanish.

Then he let the burning frenzy take him completely. He let himself become the monster that monsters fear.

And just like that, the memories vanished. He was back in the place where time had no meaning. Áine lay next to him under a perfect blue sky, her body entwined with his. Her small, warm hands caressed his chest, and her lips left a trail of kisses along his scarred cheek, then moved up to kiss the tears from his eyes.

Brendan shook with fear, pain, and regret. He didn't deserve this, this place, much less Áine. He'd been a nightmare to end nightmares. How many bodies lay in the wake of his life? But despite himself, he drew her closer and kissed over her face. Her scent was joy personified—fresh green fields after a heavy rain. Just the smell of her was like every good thing that had ever happened to him compressed into a single moment.

Was this heaven? It had to be if Áine was here, but how had Brendan gotten here? Had the Almighty taken pity on him?

No chance of that, Brendan knew, which meant only one thing. He swallowed, then lifted Áine's chin and looked deep into her eyes. It was like seeing heaven. He fought to speak the words, even though he knew the answer. "They didn't kill me, did they, love?"

Áine closed her eyes and shook her head. "No," she said. "They wouldn't let you die. You cost them too much." She kissed him then, a soulful kiss that tasted of her tears.

Brendan wept too and clung to the angel in his arms even tighter.

"But I'll be here waiting for you, *A rún mo chroí*," she whispered against his lips.

PART 2

Brendan woke, but didn't open his eyes. He didn't have the strength or desire. Physical pain greeted him like an old friend, wracking his entire body. It was nothing though compared to the hole in his chest where he longed to return to Áine. He would've wept if he had any tears left, but the oíche had beaten them all out of him what felt like weeks ago. He was still tied to the tree, his arms out and lashed with silver cord to twisted branches at the wrists, forearms, and elbows. A similar cord was around his legs at the ankle and knee. The cord around his chest was the only reason he was still upright, though it did make a deep breath impossible.

Inside, the demon was quiet and still, if it was still there at all. Whether its bloodlust had been sated, or it was just the severity of the pain and injuries that kept it quiet, Brendan didn't know. Probably the latter, since he couldn't imagine it ever getting its fill of death.

How long had it been now? Weeks? Months? Or had it just been days? The memories came back to him, and he wanted to go back to Áine. Go back and forget everything all over again. But instead he saw, in excruciatingly vivid detail, the look of terror in Caitlin's eyes just before she'd fled with Fiona. That was worse than anything the oíche or any Dusk Court fae could do to him. He didn't think he'd enough of a heart left to break, but he was wrong. How many had it taken to pull him off Fergus? Two dozen? It was all a vague smear of blood and death, screams and rage. When Fergus had disappeared, Brendan had feared the worst. But the Dark King never returned. Surely, this meant that Caitlin and Fiona had gotten away. Brendan could rest and face an eternity in hell if he knew that was true. It had to be. Fergus would never have passed up the chance to taunt Brendan with it

Yes, they had to have gotten away.

That single hope was how he bore the torture and pain. He'd won. This was just settling the debt for that escape, and he paid it gladly, much to the chagrin of the oíche. Oh, he screamed and cried out as they beat, cut, and burned him, but he never broke. Besides, when it got really bad, he got to see Áine, which was something at least.

"Wakey, wakey," said a familiar voice.

"But, Ma, it's Sunday," Brendan said through cracked, dry lips. "Can't we just—" The rest of his words were lost in a hoarse cry as the knife—his own knife—went into his side again, and twisted.

"Keep up with the jokes," the oíche said, and withdrew the blade. "It just makes this all the more fun."

Brendan opened his eyes and lifted his head to look at the oíche. Vincent looked as all oíche did: like a child born from a horror movie, all black eyes and a mouth full of pointed teeth. The dark faerie smiled and licked blood from the blade. Though he was nearly mad with thirst, Brendan managed to spit in his face. Most of it was blood.

Vincent wiped it away and smiled. "Nice try, but there is no way we're going to kill you, Fian. We've spent a good deal of effort to keep you alive." The oíche leaned in close and dragged the blade over Brendan's chest. "It was a near thing a few times, but don't you worry. These have been only the first moments of what will be a long lifetime of pain."

"What, Fergus not have the bollocks to do this himself?" Brendan asked. "I can't believe he doesn't have the stomach to watch you work."

Vincent laughed so hard he nearly fell over. "Fergus? Fergus is gone. The oíche have seized the dusk throne." He pushed the knife in between Brendan's ribs, carefully avoiding the lung, heart, and major arteries.

Brendan let out a whimpering groan, tears streaming down his face.

"The irony is, you helped fulfill our plan. Without you, and that mortal woman, we never would've been able to seize control. When she escaped, and he went after her, he was so blind with rage that he left the remnants of his power behind."

"Aye, so she made it out, then?" Brendan asked without meaning to.

Vincent nodded. "She did. Consider that bit of information our repayment for your services in our little coup."

"Aye, glad to be of help," Brendan said between pained gasps. "Why don't you let me loose and I'll show you how glad I am."

"You know, "Vincent said, cleaning his fingernails with the blade. "If you hadn't killed our brethren, we might've been willing to let you go." He shrugged. "But you did, and so here we are."

"Well then, get on with it already," Brendan said, and smiled a real smile.

"Yes, let's." Vincent put away the knife and took up a large cudgel.

It looked far too heavy for the child-sized faerie, but—Brendan felt his knee break with the first blow. He screamed in pain, though it didn't last. It was soon lost in a rush of sobbing from the torrent of follow-up blows. When Vincent finally took a moment to rest, Brendan's forearm was also broken, as were several more ribs.

"I really must thank you," Vincent said, smiling like a crazy child. "You can't imagine how therapeutic this is for me. For all of us! You should see how we all vie for our chance at you." He shrugged again, resting the cudgel on his small shoulder. "That's another reason we have to keep you alive. Don't want anyone to miss their turn."

Brendan didn't have it in him to reply.

Vincent looked him over, then let out a disappointed sigh. "Oh well, I guess we're done for today."

Something cool and wet was pressed to Brendan's lips.

"Drink."

Despite himself, Brendan did.

Vincent drew back the cup after only a few swallows. "That's enough. We don't want you dying of dehydration on us." He leaned in close and whispered, "But just barely."

Brendan licked his lips, and tasted something strange. He spit, over and over.

"Don't bother," Vincent said. "The water was dosed with it. That's just the dregs."

"What is it?" Brendan asked, but his voice was little more than a choked whisper.

"Just something to keep you from getting an infection, or even turning septic from those wounds."

"I didn't know you cared."

"Oh, more than you know," Vincent said.

Then he swung the cudgel at Brendan's head and everything went black.

Soft lips brushed over his as a small, gentle, and warm hand touched his cheek. That familiar scent washed over him and it was like he was flying; which would be fitting. She was an angel after all.

Brendan opened his eyes.

Áine smiled at him and caressed his cheek. "Hello, my love."

"I came back as quick as I could," Brendan said and made to wrap her in his arms, but he was still bound to the tree. He pulled at his bonds, but they held tight. "No, this isn't right!"

"Easy," Áine said. "You'll just hurt yourself worse." She ran her hand over his shoulders and chest. "And the oíche don't need you helping them in their work."

"Tell me true, love," Brendan said, tears he thought long spent running down his cheeks. "Is it you? Or is this some new torment?"

Áine kissed him again and again. *"A rún mo chroí,"* she whispered, her lips brushing his. "My beloved, it's me. You didn't come to me, so this time I came to you—"

A rush of wind woke Brendan with a start. He opened his eyes—though one was swollen almost shut—ready to bellow a curse at Vincent, or whatever oíche had taken Áine from him again. But something made him pause, something didn't feel right.

He looked around, scanning every shadow.

There was nothing.

Then the smell of magic hit him like a tidal wave. Not fae magic, but mortal, and more of it than he'd even known. Something about it was odd though. It smelled wild, pure, and uncontrollable. It was so vast, so powerful that he could feel it around him, like a charge of electricity in the air. But what mortal had power like that? No, that was impossible. Even if a mortal crossed over, he couldn't carry magic with him.

And yet, here it was, unmistakable. Could it be the oíche, playing a trick on him? He didn't think so. Even with Fergus's mantle of power, he didn't think they could pull this off.

That's when he smelled her. There, beneath the oceans of power that nearly blinded his senses to all else, he found the familiar smells of humanity: sweat, laundry detergent, deodorant, and—chocolate?

"It's a bleeding kid," Brendan whispered to himself.

He felt the demon inside stir. Not a raging beast, but hesitant, almost like it was afraid.

That is no child.

Brendan didn't see anyone, but he could hear the footsteps approach.

"Who's there?" he said.

The footsteps stopped and the smell of fear joined the mix of others.

"I can't see you, but I know you're there," he said.

She backed away, but her steps were light, obviously trying to be silent.

He focused on the sound and where it was. He could just see faint clouds of dust from the shuffling steps, and the root sticking out of the ground.

There was a cry of surprise as a girl appeared out of nowhere and fell onto her backside.

"Oh, shit," she said.

Brendan stared in absolute shock. She was maybe seventeen, tall and thin. Her clothes were ill fitting and clearly secondhand. Her brown hair was short and hadn't been washed in a while. She stared at him with wide brown eyes.

He just stared back for a long while, trying to figure how a child had this kind of power.

"What's your name, girl?" he asked.

She swallowed and scooted back a few inches.

"Aye, that's the smart move," he said. "I don't know where you came from, but you need to go back, right now."

No, the demon said, a silent whisper inside Brendan. *She might be able to free us and then we can finish what we started!*

"I, um, I can't," she said, getting to her feet and dusting herself off. "I mean, I can't control it."

"Jesus, girl, do you even know where you are?"

She looked around and hugged herself as she shook her head. "A haunted forest?" Her tone was sarcastic.

"Not that lucky, I'm afraid," Brendan said.

"Why are you tied up?" she asked, taking a few steps forward. She narrowed her eyes, focusing to see him in the perpetual faint light.

"That's a bit of a long story, that is," he said. "And not one to be telling a kid."

"Trust me, mister," she said. "My story isn't exactly rainbows and unicorns either."

Brendan didn't know what to say. He could see it in her eyes; hear the truth of her words. They were soaked in sadness and regret. It was something all too familiar to him.

"I have a knife," she said. "I could cut you down—Oh

my god!" Her eyes went wide when she got close enough to see his injuries. "You're hurt! Really bad!"

"Aye, I noticed that," Brendan said. "But you can't cut me loose, love. It ain't safe. Not for you or anyone else."

She kept stepping forward, her eyes looking him over. "Was it the Order?"

"The who?"

"You didn't, um, do this to yourself, did you?"

Brendan shrugged, or tried to. "Aye, though not directly."

Her face scrunched in confusion. "I have no idea what that means."

He shook his head. "It's not important. What is, is that you get your arse out of here, and right bleeding now."

"I told you, I can't control the wormholes," she said and ran her hands through her hair. "I've been jumping all over the place for what feels like weeks."

"Wormholes? What the hell are you talking about?"

She nodded. "You see, there are countless holes in space-time on the subatomic level, though I only shift through space—at least, I think." She shook her head. "Anyway, somehow I'm manipulating the chance that these holes will join together and form one large enough to reach the macro universe and—"

"I've got no bleeding clue what you're saying, girl."

"Sorry." She shrugged. "And my name's Wraith, not girl. What's yours?"

He hesitated for a long while before deciding there

was no harm in it. "Brendan," he said. "Fine then, Wraith, if you can't go back, can you make yourself invisible again? Hide until you figure out how to go back?"

"Maybe?" she said. "I mean, it just sort of happens, I don't really control it either, but I'm trying. And I'm sure I'll stride again, I always do. I just don't know when." She looked down. "But you shouldn't be close by when I do. Let's just say it would be really bad."

Inside, the demon was drawing what little strength there was and fighting for control. Brendan was pushing it back down, but he was losing.

"You have to go—"

"I told you—"

"From here," Brendan said. "From me!"

Wraith stepped a little closer, tilting her head to try and see his eyes. "Why? You're hurt really bad and tied to a tree. I don't think you could hurt me, even if I did cut you down."

"I've got no time to explain, love," Brendan said. "Trust me when I say—" There was pain as the demon fought its way up.

"I'm sorry. I was wrong," it said through Brendan's mouth. "It's the pain you see. I'm not thinking straight. Please, free me. You're right, I won't hurt you—"

Brendan pushed back, wrenching the monster from control. "Don't listen to me, go, now! Go and don't ever come back, or tell anyone you saw me!" The last thing he needed was for Dante or someone to send a rescue team. He couldn't ever go back, not with the demon unbound, and not after all he'd done.

"What? Who would I tell?" she asked, her eyes locked on his. She was scared, but also desperately curious.

Brendan grunted, and fought the demon back. "No one, I said. Just go!"

"Ah!" Jane closed her eyes and put a hand to her forehead. "Looks like you're going to get your wish. It's coming."

Brendan let out a sigh of relief, but then shuddered as he felt the magic build and build around him. It drew in, circling around Wraith like a slowly building twister.

"I'm sorry," she said, backing away. "I wish I could help—"

And before the words had even finished leaving her lips, Brendan felt a rush of that wild magic pour into him. It coursed through his body, and as it did, it began to heal him. It was a new pain. Bones came back together, mending straight, as if they'd never broken; his leg, arm, and ribs. The cuts all over his body drew closed and left not a single mark on him.

Then Wraith vanished in a whirling torrent of magic.

When the wind died, everything was silent and still again, and every single one of Brendan's wounds were healed. Even the line of runes Dante had tattooed onto his sternum to bind the demon had been restored. They'd vanished after Brendan had surrendered to the monster.

What? No!

It was chained again, but like Brendan, its strength had returned and it tore at its bonds. In fact, it felt stronger. He considered his options. Getting free now was at least possible. If he let the demon loose, it was a certainty. He could go back to the mortal world, but was there anything for him there? Dante perhaps? But Brendan knew he'd be doing the elf a favor by keeping out of his life.

No, that world wasn't his world, not anymore. He'd lived the long years after Áine's death only for vengeance. He'd done that, but now there was no escaping his true nature. Chained up or not, the demon was a part of him, of who he was. He was a monster, and a killer. He'd managed to do something good, helping Caitlin save Fiona. Better to be remembered for that.

The demon inside him howled in fury, tearing at its bonds and screaming at Brendan to let it loose.

"Easy, lad," Brendan said in whisper, standing fully on his legs for the first time in a long while. He thought of Vincent and the other oíche. "I have another bargain for you. We'll finish what we started."

Brendan made his offer and, reluctantly, the demon accepted.

It wasn't long before Brendan heard the oíche come running. He slumped down again, and bowed his head. Six oíche, Vincent in the lead, came to the site of Wraith's departure. They all stared at the huge circle of swirled dirt left behind.

"What the hell did that?" Vincent demanded.

No one answered.

"You, Fian!" he said and stepped to Brendan. "What happened?"

Brendan didn't answer. He knew his wounds were healed, but he was still covered in blood and maybe that was enough to keep the oíche from noticing.

"Let me," said another oíche.

Brendan heard him draw a knife and step closer. When the faerie was just a few feet away, Brendan raised his head and smiled. The demon surged up, filling Brendan with strength and power.

"What are you—?"

"Díoltas!"

The knife leapt from the oíche's hand into Brendan's. The second knife, flew from a sheath on Vincent's hip and into Brendan's other hand.

"Tar amach, a Bháis!"

Then there was a loud crack as the silver cords snapped and vanished from around him.

Brendan crouched on the tree branch, not moving or making a sound. He watched and listened, patiently waiting. Even the demon was still and quiet, savoring every moment of the hunt. Oíche were headed this way, four of them. Their hearts were pounding, and Brendan could smell the fear on them.

"We have to get out of here," one of them said.

"Really?" answered another. "I hadn't thought of that."

"Shut up, both of you!" said a third in a hush whisper.

The fourth didn't speak, he just led the way to the structure of white marble, which looked like nothing less than a slightly smaller version of the Parthenon. Brendan hadn't realized before, but it made sense that the hall of doors could be used to leave the Dusk Lands and even the Tír. They were usually for tormenting mortals with their greatest desires, twisting them and making them nightmares. He thought of when Caitlin had stepped through those doors. And though he never knew what she saw, it had been terrible. The second door had been so awful that she'd been forced to kill an illusion of her own daughter. How Fergus must've taken special delight in that.

Brendan leaned forward and dropped face-first from the branch. In the air he turned, bringing his feet under him and landed in the center of the oíche. Before they could react, he lashed out with his blades. There were shorts gasps, more of surprise than anything else. Then there was nothing but four clouds of darkness filled with motes of purple light.

Well done.

Ignoring the demon's praise, Brendan sheathed his knives and walked to a large oak tree. For almost two months, near as he could tell anyway, he'd hunted. Two-hundred-fifty-three Dusk Court fae had died at his hands; oíche mostly, but there were also pùcas, dusk elves, night pixies, banshees, and others. He killed them all, and he wouldn't stop until there were no more to kill. They're an evil that needed to be wiped out. There are no innocents in the Dusk Court. All of them had done terrible things to mortals through the centuries; tortured those foolish or desperate enough to bargain with them, stolen children, slaughtered lost travelers. He was bringing justice for all the mortals who'd suffered at the hands of the Dusk Court. Unfortunately, some of his prey had fled, escaped from the Tír, he knew. That was how he'd learned the hall of doors could be an exit.

And when these lands have no more prey, we will find them as well.

Again Brendan didn't answer. He just stepped to a large knot in the tree and gently traced his finger around its edge.

"Beatha?"

There was a groan and the knot opened like a cupboard. Inside was a pile of various berries and fruits and a large wood cup filled with water. Brendan took an apple and bit into it. He wasn't terribly hungry. In the Tír there was little need for food, or sleep for that matter. Unless of course the fae wanted a mortal to suffer, then they'd make the poor soul crave the food and sleep that would never come. But Brendan ate anyway. His body might not need food like it would in the mortal world, but he did need some. Of course this was all faerie food, which meant he was trapped in the Tír. The oíche had already done this of course, when they'd given him water and presumably fed him—though he didn't remember eating anything. Sure, there were ways to escape the binding. One of the fae monarchs could free him. Or he could find a powerful potion to purge the magic from him. He wasn't likely to get either, which was fine. He had no intention of ever leaving anyway.

You say that now, but the time will come.

As for sleep, he was torn. He longed to see Áine again, but not like this, not as a monster. He finished the apple in a few more bites and carried the core over to a bare piece of ground. Using his knife he dug the dry earth up, making a hole perhaps six inches deep. He dropped the core inside, covered it up, and then poured some water from the cup over it. In moments a green shoot emerged from the dirt. He stepped back as the tiny plant grew into a full-sized apple tree, complete with large apples, ready for picking.

The faeries had food stashes all over the Tír, hidden in trees and under rocks. But they weren't always easy to find, so it was good to have these fruit trees spread around. He just wished there was a way to get his hands on some meat, and then to a make a tree. His mouth watered at the thought of a steak tree.

More prey is coming.

Brendan froze and listened. He'd always had senses well beyond a normal mortal, but thanks to the demon being free, they were heightened beyond even that of a fae. Not that it mattered. Even a mortal would've been able to hear the gentle clinking of fae armor. Brendan smiled and stepped into the path, drawing his knives.

Three dusk elves, all clad in suits of scale armor with a faint purple hue to it, stepped into view. Two wore half helms, allowing Brendan to see the empty sockets where their eyes should've been. The third, clearly their captain, wore a full helm, the front etched with whirls and knots. The two each held a thin-bladed sword, unsheathed and ready. But the captain wore an ornate, curved scabbard at his hip.

"A katana?" Brendan asked.

The captain nodded once.

Brendan nodded his approval. It was true that iron, even the iron in steel, was an anathema to the fae. Just the touch of it to their skin was poisonous. But with a long and laborious process, they could enchant mortal steel, turning it to fae steel. Because it took weeks, it was reserved for only the most precious and special items.

"Go, my lord," one of the two said. "We'll hold the fian while you make your escape."

"No," Brendan said and smiled. "You won't."

The captain drew his sword and brought it up in a salute.

Brendan was taken aback, but only for a moment. He returned the gesture with his knife, offering a slight bow.

Then the fae moved as one, surging toward Brendan in a rush scarcely more than a blur. Just before their blades met, the captain leapt high while each of his guards swung.

Brendan leaned back and slid between the two, their blades passing a hairsbreadth from his face. As he went past them, he slashed out, hamstringing them both.

The two fell, crying out in pain. But to their credit,

they rolled and still tried to come at Brendan, but he'd moved out of range.

He twisted, first one way then the other, and hurled his blades at the fleeing captain who had nearly reached the steps of the hall. The fae knocked one blade aside with his katana and ducked the other, which went sailing past him and into the hall.

"*Díoltas!*" Brendan shouted.

The knife the captain had knocked aside leapt into the air and back to Brendan's hand. There was a moment where the fae knight just stared, then he realized the trap he'd stepped into. He turned, but too late. The other knife hit him in the chest, knocking him to the ground. His armor collapsed amid a cloud of darkness and twinkling dark blue lights. The knife drew itself from the armor and sped through the air to join its twin in Brendan's hand.

Brendan saluted again. "Two-hundred-fifty-four."

The two remaining dusk elves managed to get to their feet, unsteadily since they each had a leg that was useless. The wounds leaked darkness and pale grayish white motes of light.

One of the two spit at the ground. "*Díbeartach—!*"

Brendan roared in rage then flung his knives into the ground at his feet. Claws emerged from his fingertips and he was on the two remaining fae.

Two-hundred-fifty-five. Two-hundred-fifty-six.

PART 3

Wraith lay on the couch in her safe house, in almost the same spot she'd been for the last week. She hadn't slept much in that time, her dreams filled with dark memories. Even now her heart started to pound and her hands shook as she thought about how easily the room had been entered and her friends taken. Sure, she'd managed to get Geek back from the Order safely, and Con and Sprout were on the mend, but whenever she closed her eyes, she saw Ovation's lifeless body falling to the floor.

She took a deep breath, then another, and another, until her heart rate slowed and the images slipped back into the obscure corners of her mind.

It had taken her the better part of a day to clean out the furniture damaged beyond hope, and repair both the furniture that wasn't and the room itself. After fixing the holes Geek had put in the walls during the fight, she'd sealed off the literal doorway with brick and mortar. It was sloppy, but some entanglement magic had made up for her lack of bricklaying skills. The door itself now leaned against the wall; taken off its hinges, it was useless as a door-door. No one would be coming in that way again. That helped, but only a little. The room still smelled of smoke, and she could almost feel the lingering fear and pain left from the invasion. Brigid—the fae magister of the Midwestern United States—had offered to let her stay at her house. Wraith had given it a few days in the palatial one-time convent, filled with shifting hallways, soft beds, and clean clothes. But in the end, she couldn't stay. It wasn't her home. This was, or as close to one as she was going to get. So she'd worked to make it a home, trying to scrub clean the past. The last thing she'd done was to remove the extra mattresses, the ones her friends Shadow, SK, and Fritz had used. Well, she wasn't sure they'd ever really used them. It was complicated, them being dead and all, only existing because Wraith had formed bodies for them out of the quantum ether of reality. But now they were truly gone, their souls released from the binding the Order had worked. It wasn't easy, removing the last traces of her friends' existence. The mattresses didn't weigh a lot physically, but they were heavy with memories and regret. In fact, the room was still filled with both, and they soaked into her soul, leaving her grieving, depressed, and alone. She knew her friends were in a better place, but they were still gone, and she still felt their absence to her core.

Lifting her eyes from her mother's spellbook, she glanced at the shelf she'd put up—really just a board secured to the brick wall. On it sat an eagle feather, a multitool, and a pewter talisman on a black cord— the most prized possessions of Shadow, Fritz, and SK respectively. They were all she had of her friends, the only tangible things anyway. They might even be the only real evidence they'd existed at all. They were all street kids, easily overlooked and just as easily forgotten. That thought also fed the dark feelings, which wrapped her in hopelessness and sadness.

She lit a cigarette and blew out smoke.

"I really need to quit," she said to no one. "It won't be long before this whole place stinks. It probably already does."

She took another drag and let the sense of isolation wrap tighter around her. She felt more alone than she ever had before. She wasn't just missing her friends; it was also the lack of voices in her head—the countless souls the Order had bound to hers. For so long they'd been a constant torment, now she actually missed them. She even missed Nightstick. Which itself was odd. How do you miss a sentient hallucination? No, he'd been so much more than that. Then of course there was Toto, Shadow's big coy-dog, and her parents. She could still remember the accident where they'd died in the front seat of the car while she watched from the backseat, unable to do anything about it. Then she'd learned it hadn't been an accident at all. Somehow the Order had set it up to trigger Wraith's magical abilities and make her into a vessel for destructive power. But she'd brought that power back to them and wiped them out for it, freeing all—well, most—of the trapped souls at the same time. Okay, so she didn't wipe out the entire Order, but she knew she'd dealt them a blow they wouldn't quickly recover from.

On top of all that was the dream she'd been having lately (when not haunted by visions of Ovation's murder), one she was increasingly sure was a memory. Who was the guy tied to the tree? What had he done? There was something in his eyes that was clearly dangerous, but she could also see something more there, something almost familiar.

She turned her attention back to the spellbook. She found her mother's elegant script a strange sort of comfort. The formulas, or spells, or whatever they should be called, were as refined and beautiful as the lettering. As she read through each, for the hundredth time, they unfolded in her mind. She'd already read both her parents' spellbooks cover to cover a dozen times each over the past week. There wasn't even any point in reading them now, she had them both memorized. But she kept rereading them, only breaking to sleep, and that reluctantly.

And why not? Studying them was a perfect excuse to hide. Yes, she'd had plans, grand plans. She was going to start by paying the wizard the song she owed him for his help in learning the truth about what had happened to her. Then of course was her plan to reach out to the supernatural street kid community: slingers (wizards) and fifties (changelings). She was going teach them how to protect themselves, and some might even join her and help. She even had a name for the group, the Forgotten Circle.

But she never left this room. At first she told herself she just needed to clear the place out, make it her own. But the enormity of her plans kept eating at her. How could she, all by herself, do any good at all? There were so many kids out there. What difference could she make?

"If I just get better, learn better magic," she said to herself, for the umpteenth time, and went back to reading the book, analyzing every piece of every equation and how they all tied together.

Her food had run out a couple of days ago, but she couldn't bring herself to stop studying. It had become obvious very quickly that while she had power to spare, her parents were artisans, their spells clean and efficient. Wraith needed to use multiple formulas stringed together to get to a final result, but her parents had been able to distill it down to a simple, beautiful equation. They said in a few words what it took her a dozen pages to say.

That was only a small part of it though. The books were also a comfort. Seeing her parents' handwriting, reading their words, it was almost like they were still here. The first few times through the books, she'd remembered more and more, but then the memories had stopped coming. She kept trying though. It was more than a little odd how she could be consumed by a sense of hopelessness and cling to an almost obsessively desperate hope at the same time.

Her stomach rumbled, but she ignored it. Hunger was something she was long used to by now. Instead, she closed the book, set it on the floor, and stared up at the ceiling.

"What are you doing?" she asked herself. It didn't bother her that she talked and even had arguments with herself. She'd been crazy once—and probably still was, she wasn't sure—and so she'd gotten used to it. Maybe it was more accurate to say she'd gotten used to talking to a hallucination, which was basically the same as talking to herself.

"You know what I'm doing," she said. "I'm hiding and wallowing. Leave me alone."

She pulled out the cell phone Brigid had given her, and which she'd adjusted with some simple equations so it drew on the latent power all around her—thermal, kinetic, electrical, and even dark energy—and so never ran out of juice. She put her earbuds in and started the same playlist she'd been listening to over and over. The songs were perfect for fighting off dark and lonely thoughts. "Asleep" by The Smiths started playing.

She turned the music up, trying to drown out everything else. She knew the Order was still out there, rebuilding their power base, and probably still snatching kids. She closed her eyes tight and turned the music up again, trying to block out the image of Ovation dying. It didn't work, and she started to cry, again. She was sick of it all. She just wanted it all to go away.

Then a new song started. It was one she didn't know: a simple guitar and cello. The singer's voice was soft, almost sad. She glanced at the screen. "Wonder (Wonder Woman Song)" by The Doubleclicks. There was something about the lyrics, even though she knew the song was about Wonder Woman—and she'd only recently learned anything about her from Geek—it felt like the singer was speaking to her.

Never seen so many lies.

People hurting out, from the inside.

You have the strength to save us.

You have the power to know right from wrong.

She sat up and rubbed her eyes, then looked at the shelf. The singer's voice was nothing like Shadow's, but Wraith could hear her friend saying those words to her.

"But what I can do?" she asked the room. "What difference can I make?"

Ask those kids you saved what difference you made, a part of her, a voice way down deep and tinged with a southwestern accent, said.

When we're drowning in darkness, you'll save us all from going under, and we'll watch you in wonder, the singer added.

Wraith stood up and looked down at herself. Her shirt was rumpled and probably reeked something fierce; she'd been wearing it for the entire week she'd been here, and she hadn't even showered. Her eyes moved to her arms, to the mathematical formulas that marked her skin. Once, she'd thought they were tattoos, but now she knew they were the remnants of what the Order had done to her. Some of the markings had faded away, particularly those on her face and neck, but most still remained.

"No more," she said, and meant it. Maybe she couldn't completely wipe out the Order. Maybe she couldn't save every kid, but she could save one, then one more, and one more after that. She walked to the shelf and ran her fingers over the eagle feather.

"Just because you can't win, doesn't mean you shouldn't fight," she heard Shadow say.

The darkness and sadness didn't melt away, leaving her standing in sunlight, but a few rays did peek through the black clouds. Her depression was probably clinical, but at this point what was another neurosis?

She collected her parents' spellbooks and tucked them reverently into her messenger bag. She would've much preferred to have her parents teaching her themselves, but she reminded herself that she was lucky to have this much.

She pulled off her shirt and tossed it into one of two hampers against the wall. They were both magically entangled on a quantum level with matching hampers at Brigid's house in Kansas City. One was for dirty clothes, the other for clean. Brigid had insisted that if Wraith wasn't going to stay at the house, the least Brigid could do was keep her in clean clothes.

Wraith had tried not to look too eager when she said yes. There's not much to compare to clean clothes, especially underwear.

Her stomach rumbled again, more insistent this time.

"Jumping Jesus on a pogo stick," she said, looking down. "I get it, you want food."

She grabbed a can of Mountain Dew from an open case against the wall and, almost on instinct, wrapped an equation around it to draw away the heat. In a few seconds the soda was ice cold. She opened it and downed it in a few gulps. The rush of sugar and caffeine settled her stomach, a little.

"That'll have to hold you for now, buddy," she told her stomach as she walked to the clean hamper and pulled out a pair of underwear, socks, and jeans, ones that were almost the right size. That was a special treat after living so long in shoplifted thrift store specials. As she slipped off her dirty clothes and into the clean ones, she thought of Con, Sprout, and Geek. How long had it been she'd last visited? Two weeks? Three? She added a return visit to her, rather sizeable, to-do list and pulled out a long-sleeved shirt. It was black with small white letters on the front that read, "Don't mess with me, I'm good at math."

Wraith smiled. "Brigid, you are my personal faerie godmother. I'll take these shirts over a ball gown any day!" She pulled it on and adjusted it over her slender body and read the message again. "I think I have a new favorite shirt." Then she looked back to her phone, still sitting on the couch. She put the earbuds back in, put "Wonder" on a loop, and finished getting ready.

After loading up her messenger bag with everything of value: spellbooks—hers and her parents', her friends' trinkets, and the brass-and-leather glove, she walked over to the dirty hamper. She traced over the lid with her finger; as she did, the symbols and numbers drifting around her—the quantum information—floated down and settled into the equation to send her stuff to Brigid. With her laundry taken care off, she slid into her long hooded coat and set her goggles—also leather and brass—up on her forehead for later.

Dressed in all her finery, Wraith drew together the entropic formula around her, a new and improved equation she'd learned from her parents' books. This one was exponentially more efficient, and accurate, than her striding had been. Reality turned around her, but it wasn't the wild maelstrom she usually experienced; this was controlled.

When the turning stopped, she stepped from the universal junction point and into an alleyway. The sky was gray and a light misting rain was falling. She closed her eyes, smiling, and drew in a deep breath of the fresh Seattle air. She'd missed this place, though it probably didn't miss her. Not that she could blame it; she'd sort of broken it last time she'd been here. Not the whole city, but close. But she had a promise to keep, so she drew up her hood and started toward the market.

There actually wasn't a market, it not being Sunday, but somehow she knew it didn't matter. As she walked down the street, she tried not to think about the last time she'd been here. There was no sign of the murders that had happened, or of the pandemonium that had resulted when she'd lost control of her powers and manifested the shadow snatchers. Her eyes went down to the wet sidewalk and she thought of what a beautiful thing the rain was, and wondered if it might be able to wash away anything given enough time.

"I'm not telling you again," said a young, gruff voice. "This is our territory and there's a toll to cross it."

Wraith looked up and saw a group of street kids, a mix of slingers and fifties, hassling a smaller fifty kid.

"I told you, I don't have anything," said the smaller kid, a boy of maybe thirteen with pointed ears and soft, almost androgynously beautiful features. "I'm sorry, I'm just trying to get back to my squat."

"I feel for you, man," the leader of the group said in a tone that suggested he didn't. He was a slinger, an electromancer from the crackling blue lines of lightning that danced over him. "The problem is, if we let you through, we'll have to let everyone through. And we can't have that."

The group shared some snickers.

"I won't tell anyone, I promise," the smaller boy said.

"Oh, you're right about that." The slinger opened his hand and drew it back. Arcs of electricity danced between his fingers.

Wraith was on the group before anyone even knew she was approaching. She grabbed the bigger kid's wrist and twisted it, forcing him to his knees with a cry of surprise and pain. At the same time, she grabbed the metal tube of a bike rack. There was a loud pop as she used the metal rack to ground the slinger's magic.

"How'd you do that?" the slinger asked.

Wraith bent his wrist a little more, only a breath from breaking it, then she pushed him back on his butt.

He looked up at her with murder in his eyes, but when he saw her face, he went pale. "Holy shit, it's you," he said in a low whisper, rubbing his wrist.

His friends exchanged worried looks, but Wraith ignored him. She turned to the elfin fifty. "You okay?" she asked.

He stared at her with wide, luminescent blue eyes.

"Did they hurt you?"

The kid shook his head.

"Good, go on," Wraith said.

The boy went to go, but Wraith grabbed his shoulder. "Wait." She reached into her pocket where she kept the money Brigid had forced on her, pulled out a twenty, and handed it to the kid. "Get something to eat, okay?"

He smiled and nodded. "Thank you." Then he turned and hurried off.

Wraith turned to face the slinger and his friends.

"I'm sorry," he said. "We didn't know he was a friend of yours—"

Wraith knelt down and stared at the kid. "Every slinger and fifty out here is a friend of mine," she said, then shook her head. "Life's tough enough, why add to someone else's misery?"

The group exchanged confused looks.

She pulled two more twenties out and handed them to the slinger. "You guys get something to eat too."

"What's the catch?" an Asian girl, a *kitsune* fifty from the fox-like look of her, asked.

"No catch," Wraith said.

The kids exchanged more glances, but the girl took the bills.

"No more shakedowns."

The kids nodded and muttered agreement. Wraith thought they might even be sincere. She offered her hand to the slinger, and when he took it, she pulled him up to his feet. Then she walked past them and didn't look back. She thought briefly about making them the offer to join the Forgotten Circle, but the time wasn't right. They were still just bullies. Hopefully, she'd planted a seed. Maybe in time there would be something there worth feeding and growing.

When she reached an alleyway that went down into a small parking lot, she turned and followed it, though she wasn't sure what compelled her. Near the end of the alley, off to the side of some stairs leading up to Freemont Ave, a small man sat under an awning. His head was bowed, and the hood to his oversized jacket hid his face, but there was no mistaking the long gray beard hanging down his chest.

"I was starting to wonder about you, girl," the wizard said.

"I'm sorry," Wraith said and stepped over to him. "I, uh, sort of fell into a bad place."

The old man looked up at her, still as wild looking as ever, eyes full of gentle madness and wisdom. "You come to pay your debt?"

Wraith nodded. "I did."

The wizard smiled.

Wraith looked up to the symbols and numbers floating around her. She reached out and touched one, then another. With each the sound of piano keys sang in the empty air. Then she lifted her other hand and played "Moonlight Sonata," her mother's favorite song, for the wizard.

As she wove the song, literally out of thin air, Wraith thought of her mother, of listening to her play the song countless times. She could see her mother's slender, graceful fingers dance over the piano keys. It amazed Wraith how something so simple could make such a beautiful sound; each note on its own was nothing, but together the sum of the parts was more than the whole. A type of magic the world took for granted. That thought brought visions of her father, smiling at her mother with love and adoration in his eyes. Wraith lost herself for a little while, in the music and the memories.

When the last note went silent, she opened her eyes and looked down at the wizard.

"You overpaid me," he said with a smile and wiped a tear from his wrinkled cheek.

"No, I didn't," Wraith said, wiping her own tears away. "I'm just keeping a promise."

"Kid, you're bringing a smile to a lonely old man." He let out a sigh. "Sorry to say, not many show kindness these days, especially when they think we're dangerous."

She thought of the dream again. It was from when her striding had been out of control, those early days after escaping the Order. Between the cities, artic wastelands, deserts, and barren flats, she'd appeared in a forest, dark and twisted, like something out of a nightmare. A chill passed over her as she remembered the big man hanging there, bound by silver cords to the twisted tree. She remembered the pain in his bright blue eyes, the fear and desperation when he'd asked for her promise. He'd told her his name, hadn't he? She thought back, recalling the lilt of his Irish accent.

"Brendan," she whispered.

"You look like someone with a mind to do something important," the wizard said.

Wraith blinked and looked at the old man. He looked at her with sincere gratitude, so grateful for the smallest act of kindness. Then she thought of Brendan, and that look in his eye that was so familiar. How many times had she been trapped with no one to help her? Scared of herself and what she was? She knew right away what she had to do.

"Yeah," she said. "Very important."

An hour later she returned to the wizard and handed him a white paper bag. He took it and looked up at her.

"Chicken soup and a turkey sandwich," she said. "I hope you like mayo. Personally, I hate mustard."

The old man smiled and nodded. "Me too. More than just about anything."

Wraith couldn't help but beam as she adjusted the backpack straps on her shoulders. The pack was new, so its straps were stiff, and it was chockablock full.

"I'll see you later. Stay warm," she said.

The old man nodded, then pulled out his sandwich and began eating.

Wraith turned and went up the stairs to Fremont Ave. But before she reached the street, she drew up the entropic formula around her and stepped into the universal junction point.

The stride ended smoothly, though Wraith noticed it seemed to take longer than she was used to. She unraveled the swirling equations around her and stepped into the dark and twisted forest. Bare trees loomed all around her. A large full moon hung in a purple sky, marred only by the occasional cloud. She couldn't say why, but she was certain the moon was waning and that, somehow, that was significant. The silence around her was so complete, it sent shivers down her spine. Nothing moved, or even seemed alive, except for the shadows. Without thinking Wraith wrapped herself in the version of the cloak in her father's book, far more efficient and effective than her own invisibility spell.

She looked around, examining every shadow and

branch that stirred in the faint breeze. The memories of this place came back to her, disjointed and full of holes. Even so, she could tell something was wrong. Her left hand slipped inside her bag and into the leather-and-brass glove. As soon as she drew it out, the improved focus made her feel a little more at ease.

Walking cautiously down the path of old, broken tiles that were sunk into the earth—partially overgrown by dead grass—she drew together calculations of fire and force around her right hand. She didn't complete them, but held them ready should anyone, or anything, come at her. Only more silence greeted her as she stepped under the standing stones that formed a circle around the courtyard, like a Stonehenge recreation.

She froze at the scene before her. She vaguely remembered this courtyard, but it hadn't looked like this before. The marble tiles still gleamed under the light of the waning full moon, but they were all that remained intact. The rest looked like a bomb had gone off; a few of them actually.

Carefully, she avoided stepping on the countless shards of purple crystal that lay scattered over the ground. Faint and wispy threads of magic drifted off of each one, like tendrils of smoke from a smoldering fire. Her eyes moved up to what had been an intricate marble throne. Once beautiful and imposing, now it was a little more than a broken pile of rocks. Even the megaliths that made up the circle around the courtyard weren't spared. In dozens of places, four lines of deep scratches dug into the stone.

"What happened here?" she asked in a soft whisper.

It was obvious though; a massacre. The question was, had anyone survived? And who had been responsible? While she wasn't sure of the former, she was almost certain of the latter. Had Brendan been tied up because someone was afraid this would happen, or had this happened because he'd been tied up? She shook her head. It just didn't seem to fit with the man she'd talked to. There was no way she could believe this place, wherever it was, was home to warm and friendly souls. All the signs around her were of anger, a blind rage born from pain. That was something she understood all too well. Somehow she had the distinct feeling that whatever had happened here, was something well deserved.

She stepped past the remnants of the throne, through the far side of the circle of stones, and back into the twisted, nightmarish forest. Soon the courtyard was lost to shadow and haze, but she still didn't see or hear another living soul.

Knowing her destination was close, she steeled her will and tightened an equation around herself, diffusing any sound and making her effectively silent and invisible.

She reached the clearing and stared, unsurprised.

The tree was still there, but now the cords that had bound the big man hung limp, broken, and empty. The branches themselves didn't fare much better. Though they were bigger around than her thigh, they were nearly ripped clean from the tree.

Turning in a slow circle, she scanned the shadows and trees, but didn't see anything. Even so, she could feel him nearby. Despite the fear that nibbled at her stomach, she let the formula around her slip away. She thought about lowering her goggles, which would let her spot him easily if he was just hiding in shadow, but it didn't seem right. She knew the comfort of hiding in the dark, and it wasn't her place to take that away from him. Only he could, and should, do that. All the same, she did keep the entropic formula at the ready around her gloved left hand, and held the equation for force around her right.

"Brendan? Are you here?" she asked, her voice filling the empty air. But it sounded strange, like the air swallowed the sound instead of carrying it.

Still nothing moved, and despite the feeling of being watched, she began to wonder if she was wrong and he wasn't here. If she'd been hung up and then been freed, she'd have gotten as far away as possible.

Or maybe slaughter those that hung me up, she thought, remembering the courtyard and also her last encounter with the Order.

"I know you told me to go and not come back," she said, still turning in a slow circle. "But I can't do that."

Silence.

"I know you're dangerous," she said. "I could see that, and I could see you were afraid of what you might do to me." She nodded. "I know what that's like. I also know what it's like to have the deaths of innocent people marring your soul."

Still no sound or movement.

"I know what it's like to be scared of yourself and what you're capable of but can't control," she said. "I was lost and alone myself. Because of that, I won't leave someone else like that if I can help it." She pulled off the backpack and sat down, crossing her legs. "And in this case, I can."

She thought she saw a faint movement in the trees to her left. She noted it, keeping her magic ready, but didn't look that way. Instead, she just pulled out a wrapped cheeseburger and took a bite.

"I don't know how tough you are," she said between chews, "but I'm pretty tough too. I'm not as powerful as I was when we first met, but I've gotten much better control now. I don't know if I could take you, but I'm sure I could slow you down enough to get away."

A faint breeze blew by, carrying the chill of autumn nights.

She pulled a bottle of water from the backpack laden with food, water, and even a first-aid kit, then tossed the bag a few feet away. "I brought that for you. I guessed, since I didn't know what you like." She took another bite. "You didn't strike me as the vegan or gluten-free type of guy."

She took a few more bites of the burger, which was pretty good. She'd have to remember the place, and thank Brigid for the cash to get real food. After a swallow of water, she let out a deep breath and felt her stomach settle in contentment.

"You're apparently the strong, silent type," she said.

"Which is cool I suppose, but I guess that means I'm going to do all the talking." She nodded. "That's fine. I'm not normally the talkative type, but I'm in kind of a bad place, and I don't really have anyone to unload on. So, you know, lucky you."

She drank some more water and shifted her weight to get more comfortable.

"I think I told you my name," she said. "In case I didn't, you can call me Wraith. Kind of a lot has happened since I last saw you."

The words came easy, with only a break to drink some water, or get up and walk around a bit. It kind of surprised her that she wasn't more scared, but she wasn't. She talked about her friends, the Order, and everything they'd done to her. Then she started talking about her parents, everything she could remember. It felt good, like talking about them out loud somehow made the memories more solid, more real.

Brendan for his part never said a word, and Wraith never saw anything but the shifting shadows in the trees. Even so, she was absolutely sure he was there, listening to every word.

Wraith wasn't sure how much time passed, and whenever she looked up, the stars and moon seemed entirely unmoved, but she knew that was impossible. Eventually though, she just felt like it was time to go. So she got to her feet.

"This was fun, thanks," she said. "I'd offer you my number, but I bet the service here sucks. And there's the whole creeper factor." She looked around. "I'm going to take your lack of laughter as part of your laconic thing and not that my jokes are bad. I'll be back with more food and stuff. I don't know when, but it won't be long." She put her hands up and shook her head. "No, don't argue with me. You're the best listener I've ever met, so I'm just going to keep coming back and keep talking until you come out and tell me to shut up." She shrugged. "So it's up to you."

She smiled at the quiet.

"I'll take your silence as an invitation."

Nothing.

"Take care, Brendan. I'll see you soon."

She turned and was about to draw up the striding equation when something flashed in the corner of her eye. Then she saw it again, something twinkling in the moonlight as clouds passed in front of the moon's face.

She crouched down and found a battered silver pin amid the dead grass, partially covered with dirt. It was a triskelion, three interlocking spirals over a circular Celtic knot. It was strangely familiar, though she couldn't place where she'd seen it before. When it didn't come to her, she stood and held it up.

"Is this yours?"

No answer.

"Okay," she said. "I'll just keep it safe for you. If you want it back, just ask."

After a long moment, she tucked the pin into a pocket and drew up the equation around her, setting reality spinning. Before the dark and twisted lands vanished, she thought she saw a pair of blue eyes in the shadows watching her, and she could've sworn they were filled with tears.

Brendan watched Wraith vanish in a mini cyclone. Even after she was gone, he could smell magic in the air. It was still powerful and wild, but now it was more focused, less a tidal wave and more like a fire hose.

She's dangerous.

"Aye," Brendan whispered. "Aren't we all."

Brendan would've sworn the demon chuckled.

After wiping the tears from his eyes, he walked slowly to the pack, but he just stared at it. It was a large backpack and full near to bursting. He looked from the rucksack to the swirling marks left by Wraith's departure and marveled at her. After walking through hell, she came out the other side bent on being kind, on bringing more light into the world. Brendan knew full well how rare a thing that was. She didn't know him, or owe him anything, and yet . . . He looked down at the pack again. That's when he understood; she was a monster too, of a sort. That group, the Order, had made her one. Rage still churned inside him as he thought back to her telling of what they did to her. It was almost worth returning to the mortal world to find those dark bastards and show them what a real monster was.

Yes, we could avenge that girl, and her friends.

Brendan laughed without humor as he knelt down and opened the pack. "You're a force for justice and good now, then?"

*I'm the embodiment of anger and rage. As you know well,
sometimes even the furious can also be righteous.*

It bothered him when the demon made sense. He
pushed the thought aside and examined the contents
of the bag. Inside, he found two cheeseburgers. He'd
barely gotten the wrappers off before devouring them,
savoring each bite of meat. They'd grown cold, but they
were perhaps the most delicious thing he'd ever tasted.
After finishing the burgers, and licking his fingers
clean, he dug deeper into the pack. It contained dozens
of plastic pouches. Each had the letters MRE printed on
them, and a different meal name printed below that:
spaghetti and meatballs, meatloaf and mashed potatoes,
beef stew, southwestern chili, and countless others.

"Meals ready to eat?" Brendan read aloud.

There had to be two or three weeks' worth of food.
As he moved the pouches, he saw bottles of water
underneath them. He blinked and looked at the outside of the bag, then again inside. There was no way
all that should've fit inside. He reached inside, pushing pouches and water bottles aside until his fingertips
touched the bottom of the bag. His arm was in the bag
almost to this shoulder. After removing his arm, he
lifted the bag, sure it would have to weigh eighty or
ninety pounds, but it wasn't even ten pounds.

"That's bleeding deadly, that is," he said through a
smile. "A fecking magic bag."

He sat down then and began going through all the
pouches as he removed the contents of the bag. When

it was done, he had forty-five meal packs, twenty-five bottles of water (each thirty-two ounces), and a first-aid kit that could've come from an emergency room. He shook his head as he looked from the small mountain of goods and the pack that shouldn't have been able to hold a third of it. A wave of emotion surged through him, one he'd almost forgotten existed. He'd lived for so long angry and hungry for vengeance, he'd almost forgotten what kindness and gratitude felt like.

"I was wrong, love," he said quietly. "You're no bleeding monster. You're an angel to be sure."

He repacked the rucksack, slipped it on, and headed back into the woods to take his place again among the shadows.

True to her word, Wraith returned. Brendan wasn't sure how much time had passed, it had no meaning in the Dusk Lands, but from what Wraith said, it'd been less than a week. She brought another pack loaded with food and water, and four cheeseburgers this time. The smell of them almost brought Brendan out of the shadows. Almost. Instead, he sat in the darkness, ate beef stew, and listened to Wraith talk about her friends. There was a wizard kid called Con who'd had a broken arm, but his cast was off now. She brought some comic books and read them to him. They were all about Wonder Woman, an Amazon princess. Another friend, this one a changeling called Geek, had gotten her hooked on them. Brendan had always thought comic books were for young kids, but he had to admit, he liked this Wonder Woman.

"She's a Fian," he thought to himself. "No doubt about it."

Wraith also told him about a little changeling girl called Sprout who'd been hurt with Con when the Order had taken Geek and another boy called Ovation. She was apparently none the worse for wear and had adopted Wraith as her big sister. Brendan couldn't help but think of Fiona then, and Caitlin. He hoped wherever they were that they were happy and safe. Then his thoughts turned to Áine, and the darkness around him soaked into his soul. He didn't hear much else Wraith said after that, but he was still sorry when she left, and secretly hoped she'd forget about him.

She didn't. Instead, she came back again, and again. Eventually, it occurred to her he didn't have a sense of time, so she told him the date when she arrived. Once a week, sometimes twice, she came to visit and talk while he listened in the shadows. He smiled with pride when she told him how she was finding homeless wizards and changelings and teaching them how to protect themselves. He was more than a little surprised there were homeless wizard kids, and more so that they needed help protecting themselves. Then he remembered Edward, and it made sense.

"We've formed a group of sorts," she'd said. "I call it the Forgotten Circle." She laughed. "Geek wanted to call it the Justice League, but I voted that down."

Brendan smiled and listened, enjoying every word. He still wished she'd forget about him, but he was also glad when she came back. They'd even worked out a backpack exchange; him leaving an empty she'd take when leaving a full. Realizing he had more than enough food, she'd started bringing more fresh food. The empty wrappers in the bag were received as a request for more cheeseburgers, which she happily filled. Occasionally, she'd also leave in a postcard from some city or another. On each she'd write:

Wish you were here!

Your friend,

Wraith

The first had been from Dublin, and Brendan had wept quietly when he'd found it.

"So," Wraith said as she sat and opened the bag, "it's been almost three months now and you still haven't said anything. A girl could start to feel a bit self-conscious." She laughed. "It's okay though. It probably sounds odd, but these visits have been really great. I feel like you're one of my best friends, and I've only ever seen you once." She shook her head. "Anyway, I wanted to say thanks. I know you've just been sitting there listening, but I know you're there and, well, I appreciate it." She drew a bottle of golden liquid. "I don't know anything about whiskey, or even if you drink it, but I heard this was good stuff."

"No way are you old enough to be buying that on

your own," Brendan said as he stepped out of the trees.

Wraith almost dropped the bottle but didn't, for which Brendan was very grateful.

"Oh, uh, hey," she said and got to her feet. "You're, um, looking better than last time I saw you."

"Aye," he said. "Been eating these nutritious pre-packed meals for a while. Thanks for that."

Wraith smiled. "No problem. Glad you like them."

Brendan shrugged. "The vegan chili is utter shite, but the rest ain't so bad."

Wraith laughed. "Sorry, it's in the pack. I'll try to avoid those in the future."

Brendan walked very slowly toward her. Wraith watched him, and he could see the fear and hesitation in her eyes. He stopped better than ten feet away, but it was close enough to notice her looking over the tattoos and scars that covered his bare chest and arms. Up until that moment, he'd forgotten he'd been half naked all this time.

"Nice, uh, tats," she said, then cleared her throat and looked away.

"I could use a shirt next time, if you wouldn't mind," Brendan said.

Wraith nodded, but still didn't look at him. "Uh-huh, sure, no problem."

There was a long moment of silence.

"Did you steal it?" Brendan asked.

Wraith looked at him. "What?"

"The whiskey," Brendan said and nodded at the bottle.

"Oh, that." She pursed her lips and looked at the bottle. "Would you be angry if I said yes?"

"Not even a little, love."

Wraith smiled and seemed to relax a bit. After a moment of not looking at him, she realized she still had the bottle and held it out for him.

Brendan stepped forward and took it, then stepped back and looked the bottle over.

"Bloody hell," he said and smiled. "This is The Tyrconnell."

"Is that good?"

Brendan opened the bottle and took a long sniff. The smell alone was almost intoxicating. He lifted the bottle and took a sip. Warm liquid silk slid down his throat and stoked warm in his belly. He let out a long sigh.

"I guess that's a yes," Wraith said.

"Oh, aye. Well done, love. *Go raibh maith agat.*"

Wraith blinked.

"Thanks."

She smiled. "You're welcome, Brendan."

He looked at the bottle. "I'm sure you're well under age in the states, but it's terribly rude not to offer whiskey to the person what gave it to you."

Wraith eyed the bottle, then looked at Brendan. "Is it terribly rude to decline? It's nothing personal, I just don't think it's a good idea for me just now."

He shook his head. "Not rude in the slightest. Just means you're leaving more for me." He lifted the bottle, "*Sláinte,*" and took another sip.

"Well," Wraith said, "maybe it's time for you to take the lead in the conversation for a while. Now that I've plied you with drink and gotten you to come out of the woodwork." She smiled. "Get it? Wood work? Because you were in the trees?"

"I think I need another drink."

"Not one for puns, huh? Duly noted."

Brendan let out a breath, looked around, then sat down. "All right, fair play. Least I can do is a bit of talking for a change."

Wraith beamed and sat down, crossing her legs, and leaned forward.

"Have you ever heard of the Fianna?"

THE LEGION OF SOLOMON

"Nice day, huh, Collins?" Mitchell, the Humvee driver, asks me. He's a few years older than me, which means just old enough to have beer back home. The guy is about as average as you can get, which includes his sense of humor.

I give him a flat look. "Yeah, it's only 108 today, and we haven't taken any fire in an hour. I love spring in Iraq."

"Yeah, but it's a dry—" Mitchell starts to say, but the collective groan shuts him up.

"Don't forget about the sand in all your nooks and crannies," Johnson says from the turreted fifty-caliber. "Three tours here and I still can't figure out how it gets in. Swear to God, I used duct tape over my skivvies once. Didn't do a damn bit of good."

We all waited for the punch line.

"Of course it did provide a new method of getting my regular Brazilian waxing in."

We all laugh, and the tension eases, but just a little. Johnson is the funniest bastard I've met since getting deployed. He's tall, has a shaved head, and is 250 pounds of solid muscle. I'm convinced there's a defensive line somewhere that sorely misses him. Dude is also the best shot with any weapon he puts his hands on, which is why he's on the fifty.

I've only been in the sandbox a few months, but that's long enough to know you have to laugh, especially on these convoy missions. I don't know how Johnson's done this for three tours. Almost five years.

Everyone goes quiet as we move into the city. The streets are deserted, which is never a good sign.

"I wish we had one of those V-hull rigs the marines get," I say under my breath.

"Stow the chatter," Sarge says over the radio. "Hold up here, I don't like the look of—"

It all happens so fast.

The lead Humvee goes up in a ball of flame, someone yells "IED!" over the radio, and then the gun truck goes up. After that, it's all sporadic gunfire, and more explosions all around us. It becomes a full-on Charlie Foxtrot in record time. That's the alphanumeric for the letters *C* and *F*. For the civilians, the *C* stands for cluster. You can figure out the *F*.

Then everything goes black.

"Kid, can you hear me?" someone asks.

I can hear the voice, but it's miles away. My brain is

a jumble. I'm not sure where I am or what's happening, but I know I shouldn't be lying down, or sleeping, or whatever the hell I'm doing. Sarge will kick my ass if he catches me.

Why the hell can't I get up?

"Nonresponsive," someone else says.

"Three, Six, provide cover. We'll get the wounded inside," the first voice says.

His tone is one I know well, a commanding officer. Even in my brain-scramble, I find myself trying to follow his orders.

"Yes, sir," two voices say in unison.

"Four, soon as we're in, I want wards up."

"Copy that."

"Move, now!"

At first I think maybe this is an exercise. But only until someone grabs the drag handle on my vest and hauls me across the rough ground. Pain surges through my body, worse than anything I've ever felt, and I hear someone cry out. A moment later, I realize it's me.

I'm almost sure I learned in my training that that's not good.

It takes all my focus, but I manage to kick my brain into gear and open my eyes. The world is a stuttering blur of dust and dirt and blood and fire, like a movie with half of every second frame missing. There are two guys, I think they're friendlies, but they're not wearing standard Army Combat Uniforms. Their ACUs are all black. They're taking cover behind a seriously mangled Humvee, but they're not holding any weapons. I see the rest of my detail all around me. None of them are moving, some of them aren't even whole. A few of those who are, are being dragged by more of the men in black.

In an odd moment of clarity, my brain latches onto my training when I spot a rifle. I grab it, though the movement sends even more pain through me.

I look back to the two taking cover behind the Humvee wreckage just as I'm being dragged into a building. I'm pretty sure no one uses flamethrowers anymore, and I don't see a tank on either guy's back, but one of them is spraying a jet of flame forty feet long out of his hand. They must be spec-ops, right? Some kind of new weapon system the grunts haven't seen yet? All things considered, it shouldn't be surprising if they had three heads.

As I'm dragged over a doorway, my body bounces. I wince and grit my teeth. For a moment, everything goes white and I have to fight to get my senses back. But I never let go of my rifle.

Sarge would be proud of that much, at least.

Where the hell is Sarge?

I hear a voice through the pain.

"Can you hear me, kid?"

I nod, since I can't seem to get anything out from my clenched jaw. It feels like a month before I get the upper hand on the agony running through me. Someone props me up against a wall. I take a slow breath, then open my eyes. I'm in one of the many buildings lining the street; old and gutted, typical for this area of Iraq.

"I know that look," a voice says, and I recognize it as the one giving orders outside. "That's a good sign, son."

I look up and see one of the guys in black ACUs standing over me. I hadn't noticed it before, but he has a hood as part of the uniform, so all I can see are some scars.

"You're hit, but it's not bad. We're gonna take care of you. Don't worry," he says.

"My squad?" I ask.

"Looks like three others are alive. They're in rough shape, but I think they're going to make it if we can get an evac."

He doesn't mention the other six. I don't have to ask what that means.

"Who are you guys?" I ask through gritted teeth. Anger is making it easier to push back the pain and I'm noticing more details around me. I scan his uniform for patches. There's no branch or rank detail. There's just a unit patch, but it's nothing I recognize. It looks like concentric circles with a star inside and a bold "1" in the center of it. The space between the circles is filled with odd script I don't recognize. I think the star is a Star of David, but I didn't think the Israelis had anyone here. But these guys sure sound like Americans. I look, but don't see a flag patch anywhere.

"We're friendlies," he says, noticing me checking his uniform.

I haven't been out of boot long, but I know "you don't need to know" when I hear it. I'm also smart enough to know when to shut up and appreciate someone pulling your ass out of a fire, especially a literal one.

I almost jump out of my skin when I hear what sounds like a freight train strapped to an A-10 outside. It's followed by an explosion that shakes the whole building. Dust falls around me, and I grip my rifle, waiting for the walls and roof to follow suit.

The team leader moves away, speaking into a throat mike and listening to an earpiece, but I don't see any cords or radios on him. I look around and see four others, all in the same black, hooded uniforms. One is, well, it looks like he's drawing something on the walls with white chalk, more circles and strange letters. The other three move out of the room, back out the way we came in. I look away, and that's when I see Johnson, Mitchell, and the Sarge lying nearby. They're not moving, and they're covered in blood. Johnson's right arm looks mangled, and his face is burned. I can't bear to look at him for long. I look at Sarge. He's cut up and burned too. I just stare for a long while. He's in his forties, late forties, with weathered brown skin that looks more like leather, and he's the toughest man I've ever met. I sort of expected bullets and shrapnel to just bounce off him. Seeing him like this does more to rattle me than anything else so far.

I check my rifle and my ammo supply. Weapon status red, ready to fire. Deep breath. I've got two magazines on me. Not much ammo, but I'll make it count.

"Get Three and Six in here," the team leader says over the sound of gunfire outside. "Then I want full wards up around the room. All elements covered, just in case those bastards have a mystic with them."

"Yes, sir," says the one drawing on the walls.

There's the sound of a huge electrical arc followed by a boom of thunder that shakes the building again. I move to cover Sarge from the falling dirt from the roof, but my body doesn't respond.

Moments later the team reassembles on the far side of the room. I count seven of them, and notice each has a different number on his unit patch.

"Sitrep," the team leader, who has a "1" on his patch, asks the one with a "4" on his.

"The rest are angel, sir," he says. "I count at least five IEDs used, all Monday, and at least a dozen RPGs. These guys didn't have a chance. This was a damned meat grinder. Frankly, it's a miracle any of them are still—"

I grit my teeth. "You don't have to talk like I'm not—"

"Settle down, soldier!" One says. He looks at me, then at my name tape. "Collins. I'm sorry for your squad, but you're in the middle of shit you can't even begin to process, son."

His tone does more to shut me up than the words themselves.

"We're going to do everything we can to get you and your squad out of here, all of them. But you need to sit back and let us do our job." His eyes go hard and bore into me. "Do you understand me, Private?"

"Yes, sir," I say more out of instinct. In a moment

of panic, I'm back in basic training and calling the drill sergeant "sir." One doesn't glare or scream at me that he works for a living, so he's probably an officer.

He nods, then turns back to his team. I can hear them speaking, but it's too quiet for me to make out now. And that's when I notice something missing from their gear, and my stomach drops through the floor.

"Christ, you don't have any weapons!" I say without thinking. None of them has so much as a side arm.

One glares at me, and I go silent again. I can't tell you why, but I now know this guy doesn't need a rifle, or any kind of gun, to bring a world of hurt down on someone. I think he could call an airstrike from sheer force of will. He scares the shit out of me, and he said he was a friendly.

"Are the wards up?" One asks without looking away from me.

"We're sealed tight," Four, the one who'd been drawing on the walls, says from the doorway.

I blink and stare, but nothing changes. The odd writing that covers the walls now also covers the doorway, but there's no door, so the symbols just hang in the air.

What the hell are you guys? I want to ask, but have enough sense not to. I'm dense, but I eventually learn.

One nods, then walks over and crouches down to look me in the eye. "Listen up, Collins. I don't know who the hell sent your convoy through here today, but rest assured I will make sure they receive an ass-chewing about which epic poems will be written. But you're here, we're on the same side, and we're gonna help."

"I sense a monster *but* coming, sir," I say.

He nods and smiles a little. "But, you can't ask any questions. Suffice it to say, we don't exist." He looks at me for a long while. Through the shadow of his hood, I see his dark eyes; they almost look to be filled with swirling white clouds. "Try not to move. Our medic is gonna see to you and your squad, then we'll try to get you out of here."

"Yes, sir," I say. When in doubt, shut up and follow orders.

He stands, turns to Two, and nods at Sarge. "Check him first."

"On it," Two answers, then pulls a bronze pedant with a vividly clear and bright blue stone set in the center from a utility pouch. He wraps the long chain, of the same metal as the pendant, around his hand a couple of times and crouches over Sarge. With care and gentleness that seems at odds with the circumstances, he places the pendant on Sarge's chest. A blue light surrounds the still form of the massive man who put the fear of God in me every day, and who I thought was invincible.

A moment later, I remind myself to keep breathing.

"Shrapnel in eight places, second- and third-degree burns, and some internal bleeding," Two says. "I can stabilize him." He closes his eyes and slowly turns the pendent. After a moment, the blue glow around Sarge gets a few shades lighter. Two smiles and opens his eyes. "Check, he should be okay."

"Good," One says, then turns to Five. "Any sign of Sierra Novembers?"

"That's a negative, sir," Five says from a window, a hint of Louisiana bayou in his voice. "I see Monday forces only."

I stare, trying to make sense of what I'm seeing, but I can't. Five is just standing there, right in front of the window with no cover at all. But somehow, he isn't drawing any fire.

I dig through the addled recesses of my brain to try and remember if I've heard of Sierra Novembers before.

I look at Sarge, still glowing, and the pendant on his chest. Then I think back to the flamethrower. That's when I realize that Five wasn't saying "Monday" like the day, he was saying "mundane." A chill runs through me and I start breathing fast. This has to be the result of serious head trauma. Or a dream, a truly messed-up dream. I feel One's eyes on me. When I look up at him, I figure it out, and the words just pop into my head. I'm not able to meet his eyes, but I know I'm right. Sierra Novembers: supernaturals.

In the middle of shit you can't even begin to process, he'd said. Talk about the understatement of the century.

"This one is in rough shape," Two says as he looks over Johnson. "Aside from a shattered humerus, he knocked his head pretty bad, possible cerebral hemorrhage. I'm going to pause him till the mundane medics can get here. Even so, we need to get him clear."

I watch as he traces his finger over Johnson's chest,

leaving white symbols behind like glowing finger paint.

"They're closing around us," Five says.

"Sir, if I can get on the roof, I can rain some flame down and thin the buggers out," says the one with a British accent and a "3" on his patch.

One nods. "Light 'em up."

Three turns and runs out of the room.

"This one isn't so bad."

I see Two kneeling over Mitchell. Two pulls another pendant out, this one silver with a yellow stone in the center, and sets it on Mitchell's forehead. "Just blast damage, he'll be fine." Two stands and comes over to me.

"What'd you do?" I ask, looking at the others. Sarge still has a glow on him, Johnson still has the symbols on him, and now Mitchell seems to be glowing like the Sarge, but instead of blue, he's yellow.

"No questions, soldier. You heard One." I see a smile from the shadows of his hood. "Hold still." He passes a hand over me.

I feel a jolt of cold and flinch. I haven't felt cold since I got to the sandbox. I'd almost forgotten what it felt like.

"Three, no, four broken ribs, pulled muscles, and some light shrapnel damage to your left deltoid," Two says. "Do you feel any pain?"

"A twinge here and there," I say through clenched teeth.

He chuckles. "Okay, just keep breathing, that's the secret to staying alive, you know." He reaches into another pouch and pulls out a green clump. It looks like something a horse would leave behind. He pushes it to my mouth. "Eat this."

"It looks like horse shit!" I protest.

"Tastes like it too, but it isn't. It'll help with the pain." He holds it in front of my mouth.

After a bit of consideration, I decide that even if it is horse shit I don't care, as long as it helps the pain. I open up and he pushes it in. I've never tasted horse shit, but it's how I imagine it'd taste. I swallow and immediately, truly immediately, I feel the pain fade. I look at Two, dumbfounded.

"Told you," Two says and stands up. "Causalities are treated and stable, sir."

"Good," One says. "I imagine this is confusing as all hell, Private. The only thing I've been cleared to tell you is we're with the American military. I'm One, that's Two, our medic. Three is on the roof with Seven, and that's Four, Five, and Six." He motions to the three other men in the room, who nod in turn.

"How many of you are there? Can I ask that, sir?"

"Seven, always seven," One answers.

"Well, I'm glad you were there, sir. We'd be dead by now if you hadn't been."

One doesn't answer, he just nods. It's obvious he's still upset we were here at all, but that's one ass-chewing that's above my pay grade, thankfully.

After a few minutes of sitting quietly, I decide to try

getting to my feet. I move slowly, waiting for the pain to hit me, but it never does.

"Whoah! Take it easy," Two says, coming to me. "Just 'cause you don't feel it, doesn't mean you're healed."

"I can't sit here anymore, sir," I say. "Please."

One nods and Two helps me stand. I walk to the window and look out. It's the first I've gotten to see the situation. The line of Humvees are still burning and nothing but a barely recognizable pile of twisted metal. I try, and fail, not to see the bodies still in them. I turn from the scene, trying not to notice the smell. That's when I see a small group of hostiles come around a corner. On instinct, I raise my weapon.

"You don't see me. I'm invisible to you," I whisper and feel a familiar sensation of pressure around me.

When they look my way, I put my finger on the trigger and watch them closely.

They seem to look right through me. No one shoots, or even raises their weapon.

"Hold fire," One says.

"Sir?"

"I said hold fire," One says again. "You open up and it'll draw them right to us."

The hostiles continue by like I wasn't twenty feet away with them in my crosshairs. When I look up at One, he and Two are staring at me.

"What were you whispering?" One asks.

I shrug. "I call it my Jedi mind trick, sir. It's stupid. Just something I do."

"If it's stupid why do it?" Two asks.

I look from him to One and back. "I don't know, sir. Superstition I suppose. Sometimes it seems to work."

"Like it just did?" One asks.

I furrow my brow. "That was your doing, wasn't it, sir? I've seen others of your team standing in clear view too."

"Can't say," One says, but he's smiling a little now. "Sorry."

He and Two exchange a glance, and I can tell there's an entire conversation behind it, but I'm smart enough to keep my mouth shut. Not that it matters because at that moment I see flashes of red out of the corner of my eye. I flinch back behind cover. When I peek around the window's edge, I see small streaks of flame raining down from the sky into the street. They look like little comets, dozens of them. The hostiles that just went by come running back and join a larger group. The meteor shower pours on them, each little comet exploding on impact. The blasts send the hostiles flying in all directions.

Soon there are shouts coming from all around us and I see more of the mini fireballs raining down behind other buildings.

"Who's your radioman?" One asks me.

"Sir?" I ask, not looking away. My brain doesn't seem able to accept what I'm seeing. It must be some kind of new air support weapon, but I don't hear any planes overhead.

"Your radio," he asks again, more force in his words. "Who has your radio?"

My head snaps back to him and I answer without thinking. "Cruz, sir. Lance Corporal Cruz."

"Four, Six," One says.

"Sir?" they answer in unison.

"We're out of time," One says. "They're starting to close in, we need to evac the wounded. Get out there and see if you can find that radio, and if it's still operational."

"Yes, sir." They exit the room and I watch as they emerge on the street moments later.

"Step back from the window, son," One says.

"Sir?" I ask.

"You're not cleared for what you'll see, Private," he says.

"What are—" I don't get to finish my sentence. I hear gunfire outside. I instinctively take cover, but can't keep myself from looking back, peeking around the window. I see a group of hostiles come from around the corner and open fire. Four, I think, moved his hand in a circle and the bullets actually curve around him, striking nearby buildings. Six punches the air in front of him. Two cars are hurled through the air as if kicked by a giant, landing on the hostiles.

"Holy shi—!"

"Collins, step away from the window," One says again with all the authority of God speaking to Moses.

I turn away. "Sorry, sir."

When I look up, One has pulled his hood back. He looks to be in his early fifties, which means he's probably early forties. Military men age hard. His face bears the lines of every hard mile, and his brown hair is peppered with gray. His eyes are hard, made of military-grade steel, just like the rest of him. I imagine this guy could take apart half a dozen men years his junior

"This isn't some new tech, is it, sir?" I ask.

"I can't answer that," One says. "We're called the Legion of Solomon, and you're going to be told in your debriefing that you never saw us."

I nod. "Yes, sir. But how—?"

He doesn't blink. "You heroically pulled your squad mates into shelter and held up here until help arrived. You'll probably get a medal."

I'm not a genius, but I'm able to figure out just how much slack he's cutting me, so I step back from the window and nod. "I understand, sir."

"Bloody hell, contact left!" says a clipped British voice, soon followed by Three barreling back into the room. "Sierra Novembers, sir! We're live."

"What do you have?" One asks.

"Mystics, sir, two of them," Three says. "I caught their smell, then I saw them. They're leading a group of about ten insurgents, all mundanes. Bloody mystics must've figured out how to hide from us."

"We need to get clear of this building. They'll bring it down on top of us if we stay here," One says. At that moment Four and Six come back into the room.

"The radio?" One asks.

"Right here, sir," Four says holding it up.

"Huddle up," One says.

Five and Seven enter the room and everyone gathers around One.

"Here's the deal. We've got incoming hostiles: two mystics, probably working in tandem, and ten mundanes, probably followers."

There's a round of muttered curses from the team.

"If there's two in tandem," Five says, "we might have a jinn to deal with too."

"We've dealt with them before," One says, then turns to Two. "Get the best ward you can over the wounded."

Two nods.

"Five and Six, you two get them off the ground so we can move them fast," One says, then looks at them hard. "You make sure they don't get hit again, you hear me? We've got enough angels today."

Both men nod.

One continues. "Since we're moving, the wards won't be as strong. When they're up, you each move one of the men. Two, you get the one on pause." He turned to another team member. "Three, you call for a med-evac, no delays. I want birds in the air before you hang up, got me? Authorization Alpha-one-one-Foxtrot."

"Done and done," Three says.

I can't stand sitting on the sidelines anymore while the grown-ups make plans. It's probably stupid, but I step forward. "What can I do to help, sir?"

"This is out of your league, kid," Seven answers. I can't see his face, but I feel his glare.

"Besides, you're hurt," Two says, more gently. "Even if you can't feel it."

"Sir," I say to One, "with all due respect, this is what's left of my squad and I can't just sit on my hands. What would you do in my position?"

One takes a deep breath, then looks me up and down. After a moment he turns back to his team. "Okay. Three and Four, you're with me. We focus on those mystics and bring them down. Hit hard and fast, don't give them a chance to breathe."

"Yes, sir," both men answer.

"Collins." One turns to me. "Get what ammo you can off your buddies, and keep an eye out for any loose magazines outside. Don't spend much time scrounging, focus on the mund—the insurgents."

"Yes, sir." I pick up my rifle and check it again.

One is saying something to the others while I check Mitchell, Johnson, and the Sarge for ammo. Johnson and Mitchell are dry, but God bless Sarge. He has four mags stuffed in various pockets.

"Everyone ready?" One asks.

"Hooah," I say.

Two, Five, and Six move over to Johnson, Mitchell, and Sarge and gesture over them. The three still forms slowly lift off the ground, stopping at about two feet.

I stare like an idiot for a few second, remembering back to being six and playing "light as a feather, stiff as a board." Then I push it down and get my head in the game. I have no idea what's happening around me, but I know my buddies need me and I'm not going to let them down.

Two, Five, and Six each draw something on the chests of the floating men. When they seem happy with whatever it is they've done, the three of them move toward the door. The three injured, unconscious men float behind them like tethered balloons.

Somewhere in the back of my head I'm thinking how messed up it is that this is the best story ever and I'll never be able to tell it to anyone.

"Move, now!" One shouts.

We burst from the doorway, and everything slows down.

A group pops around the corner a few buildings down. I see nearly a dozen with AKs and two in the front wearing *thawb* robes. They look unarmed.

I take aim and open fire on the ones with the AKs. I drop a couple before the others return fire.

One throws his hand forward and I feel my hair stand up. There's a cracking sound and a huge lightning bolt, at least it looks huge to me, leaps from his hand, striking one of the robed figures. The bolt sends the man flying several feet, tumbling in the air like a rag doll. The bolt then forks, hits two hostiles' weapons, and surges through them into the men themselves. The other robed figure makes a motion, and as a fork heads for him, he deflects it into the ground.

I take cover when the return fire starts, some of which happens to be actual fire.

When there's a lapse, I pop out and lay down suppressive fire of my own, though mine is strictly the 5.56-millimeter-copper-alloy-slug variety. I'm a little surprised how calm and focused I am. Don't get me wrong, I'm not raw, but I still struggle to keep it together under fire. Not today though.

"Go," One says. "Get the wounded to the extraction point!"

Three sweeps his hand out in front of him. A gust of wind blasts the ground, sending sand up and forward in a cloud.

"Incoming!" a Legion team member shouts.

I look up in time to see a fireball come screaming through the conjured sandstorm. I leap for cover and feel a stab of pain. Guess the horse shit is wearing off.

There's an explosion, the blast of it makes my landing less than graceful, and I feel heat on my back. When I turn over, the building we just left is blasted to rubble.

One orders us back. I empty the last of my mag into the group, drop it, and load another as we back away in a covering pattern.

When we start taking fire from a nearby building, Six steps into the street. He brings his arms up and then down quickly. I feel my stomach lurch, like I'm on a roller coaster doing a loop. The building collapses like a can being crushed underfoot.

The fight goes on like that for what feels like weeks, but is probably less than a couple of minutes. I take cover, fire, take cover, fire. All the while the Legion boys toss fire, lightning, air, and sometimes buildings or cars. I lose track of how often I fire, and reload, until I hit my last mag. I focus, conserving my ammo for good shots as we continue our retreat. I can't even see the three wounded, but that's a comfort. That means they're behind me and closer to the extraction. The last robed figure steps out and hurls a ball of what looks to be just pulsing light. One leaps forward and sweeps his arm out. The light bounces off something and hits a building. There's a flameless explosion and the building shatters into dust. The shockwave hits me, indirectly, but that's enough to scramble my brain and send me ass-over-teakettle.

"Drop that bastard!" One says.

One, Three, and Four move to the street as I get my sense back. I take shots at any hostile who gives me a target.

One makes an X out of his arms then opens them quickly as Three and Four both drive their fists into the ground. A giant hand of sand and stone reaches up from the ground and grabs the mystic. The giant fist tightens.

Without thinking, I take aim and open fire, three quick shots. There's a red spray as the body jerks in the earthen hand. In a moment, the hand collapses and the mystic's body follows suit.

Someone screams a phrase I know all too well. I take cover just as the hostiles begin their death blossom: opening fire on full auto in our general direction.

I hear the bullets zip by and hit the wall behind me. When I look up, I see my wounded squad a few feet away, but they're on the ground and there's no sign of the Legion.

Panic hits me as I realize I'm alone and hopelessly outnumbered. It might've started at ten, but some passersby must've join in because I hear what must be twenty voices screaming at me.

"Hell with it," I say. I pop up and fire.

My rifle barks twice then goes silent.

I take cover again, and try to figure out my options. It doesn't take a genius to know I've run dry. I hear them in the street taking position to move on me.

I toss my rifle and grab my side arm. It's better than nothing, and at least I'll go fighting. A couple of deep breaths to steady my nerves and I listen; I have to let them get close.

That's when I hear a loud barking, and I smile like a kid on Christmas at the beautiful, familiar sound of a Browning M2 .50-caliber machine gun opening up. It's joined by the chopping sound of Blackhawk helicopter blades.

I look and see four Humvees rolling down the street toward me. The two in the front are laying down lines of fire. I sit on the ground, back against the wall, and start laughing. I look at Mitchell, Johnson, and Sarge. The pendants and glowing writing are gone. At this point, I'm not even sure I didn't just imagine the whole thing.

"Private, you hit?"

A medic is standing over me.

"I'm okay for now, get them in first," I say, motioning to the three on the ground.

In seconds, the three are on stretchers and loaded

in the back of the Humvees. I go to stand and all the pain that was gone just minutes before is back, with a vengeance. In fact, I'm having trouble breathing.

"Lie down," another medic says to me. Still another runs up with a stretcher. I know I can't stand so I start to do as he says. Then the pain overwhelms me and I fall over. They move quickly, getting the stretcher under me.

All I see is dark sky and I feel myself being bounced as they load me into the Humvee. I manage to turn my head and see Mitchell on my right.

"We've got them, move out," I hear someone say. We lurch forward and speed down the road.

"What happened?" I hear someone ask.

"Ambush," I say. "IEDs, RPGs, lots of fun for all."

"Don't worry, brother, we got another team rolling in for the rest of the convoy. We won't leave them out there," the voice says.

"How'd you hold them off?" another voice asks.

I take a deep breath and feel stabbing pain. "I can't tell you."

"It's all right," the first voice says. "It's common to have holes in your memory after something like that. You saved your buddies' lives though."

"Hope so" is all I can say.

"You'll probably get a medal out of this."

"That's what I hear." It had to have been real, right? I couldn't have hallucinated something like that.

"Fritzy, you hear thunder?" the voice asks.

"I think so, but there isn't a cloud in the sky."

"Man, there's some seriously weird shit going down today," the first voice says.

"You got no idea," I say too quietly for anyone to hear. I look over at Mitchell. "You're lucky you'll miss out on the debriefing. That's going to be fun."

ACKNOWLEDGMENTS

First and foremost, thanks to you, the readers and fans of the American Faerie Tale series. There are truly no words to express my gratitude. To the Knights of Powahatan for your continued support, friendship, and encouragement: Kenda, Mike, Dustin, Kristin, Casey, Geoff, AND Baby G. Thanks to Angela and Aubrey (The Doubleclicks) for making music that inspires, entertains, provokes thought, and redefines the word "awesome." As always, thanks to Rebecca, my editor, even though you got off really easy this time. Thanks to my Harper Voyager Impulse colleagues, we might not be keeping each other sane, but we are keeping each other less insane.

ABOUT THE AUTHOR

BISHOP O'CONNELL is the author of the American Faerie Tale series, a consultant, writer, blogger, and lover of kilts and beer, as well as a member of the Science Fiction & Fantasy Writers of America. Born in Naples, Italy while his father was stationed in Sardinia, Bishop grew up in San Diego, CA where he fell in love with the ocean and fish tacos. While wandering the country for work and school (absolutely not because he was in hiding from mind controlling bunnies), he experienced autumn in New England. Soon after, he settled in Manchester, NH, where he writes, collects swords, revels in his immortality as a critically acclaimed "visionary" of the urban fantasy genre, and is regularly chastised for making up things for his bio. He can also be found online at A Quiet Pint (aquietpint.com), where he muses philosophical on life, the universe, and everything, as well as various aspects of writing and the road to getting published.

Discover great authors, exclusive offers, and more at hc.com